LEAH'S IRISH H

Slick Rock 4

Becca Van

MENAGE EVERLASTING

Siren Publishing, Inc.
www.SirenPublishing.com

A SIREN PUBLISHING BOOK
IMPRINT: Ménage Everlasting

LEAH'S IRISH HEROES

ISBN: 978-1-62241-066-8

First Printing: June 2012

Cover design by Les Byerley

Printed in the U.S.A.

PUBLISHER
Siren Publishing, Inc.
www.SirenPublishing.com

DEDICATION

To anyone in need of a hero or two.

LEAH'S IRISH HEROES

Slick Rock 4

BECCA VAN

Chapter One

"Oh my God," Leah muttered.

Leah Harmer looked up as the bell above the diner door rang. She froze in her tracks as she watched two of the sexiest, tallest, most handsome men she'd ever seen walk through the door. They were sex on legs and oozed confidence. The shorter of the two had crew-cut blond hair, blue eyes, wide muscular shoulders, muscular pecs she could see rippling beneath his tight white T-shirt, a slim waist, and the longest, strongest thighs she'd ever seen under a pair of worn denim blue jeans. He looked to be around six foot four, two hundred pounds, and maybe a few years over thirty. He moved with the grace of a feline predator.

She slid her eyes to the man slightly behind him and off to the right. He was even bigger. He had to be at least six foot six, around two hundred ten pounds, and he had to be at least thirty-five. His biceps bulged under the seam of his black T-shirt, making her panties damp. He was dark, the complete opposite to the other man's light coloring. His hair was also crew-cut short, but it was black. His eyes were a deep, stormy gray, his shoulders nearly as wide as the door he'd just passed through, and she could see his cut abs through his tight shirt. His waist was slim, as were his hips, and his thighs were nearly as big and tree trunks. She could see his quads rippling beneath his black denim jeans as he moved.

Leah couldn't take her eyes off of them. She felt her breasts swell, her nipples pucker, and her pussy clench as fluid leaked onto her panties. She looked up and up and up as the two men stopped in front of her and she met their eyes.

Blondie reached out and pushed against her chin with a large finger, closing her mouth with an audible snap. Leah felt her cheeks heat and knew she was a red as a fire truck.

"Hi, darlin', do you think we could get a table?" Blondie asked.

Leah felt her cheeks heat even more, turned, and led the two men over to an empty booth. She kept her eyes lowered and hoped they didn't see the way the man's lyrical Irish accent had affected her body. Her nipples were rasping against her bra, and she could hear her own elevated breathing.

"Wh–What can I get you?" Leah asked.

"I'll have a burger with the works, fries, and coffee," Blondie ordered.

"I'll have the same, thanks," the dark-haired man replied.

"I'll be right back," Leah squeaked and scurried off to the kitchen.

She leaned against the doorjamb and tried to gather her wits. *God, what is wrong with me? I fall to pieces at the sight of two large, sexy men, and just after getting over my crush on Damon. Am I so fickle?*

"Leah," Earl, the owner of the diner, called out to her as he worked the grill. "What are you doing just standing there, girl? Get your ass moving."

"Sorry, Earl. I need two burgers with the works with a side of fries."

"Okay, that order will be next, now get this meal out to table five," Earl barked as he placed the ladened plates in the serving window.

Leah took a deep, steadying breath and headed back out the door. Leah served the food and then she grabbed one of the warming pots of coffee off the large hot plate, poured two mugs, and took them over to the two Irish gentlemen.

"Thanks...Leah," Blondie said after his eyes had drifted to the name tag pinned over her left breast.

Leah turned to leave but was stopped when a large hand wrapped around her wrist. She turned back to see the two men eying her with hunger. She felt her cheeks heat again and wished she could hide in the kitchen until they left. She hadn't blushed so much since she was a kid. She was totally out of her element and had no idea how to handle it.

"How old are you, Leah?" asked Blondie.

"Twenty-three."

"Hm, have you lived in Slick Rock long?" the dark-haired man asked her.

"Um, what's with the inquisition?" Leah asked, pulling her wrist out of Blondie's grasp.

"Just curious. My name's Seamus O'Hara and this is my brother, Connell."

"Leah, get your fat ass over here, now," Earl yelled through the serving window.

Leah jumped and rushed over to the window. The fury on Earl's face when he was talking to her was nothing new. The man had been mad at her ever since she'd turned down his request for a date. His bark was much worse than his bite though, thank goodness.

"Stop fraternizing with the customers and get back to work, gal, or you're gonna find your ass out on the street." Earl growled at her. He shoved the order of burgers and fries into her hands.

Leah scowled at Earl but took the order and headed over to where the O'Hara brothers sat. She placed the food before them on the table and spun on her heel, ready to head back to the kitchen. A massive hand gently closing around her wrist halted her in her tracks. She looked over to Connell and saw the anger in his eyes.

"Does he always treat you like that?" Connell asked.

Leah looked away from the big man and shrugged her shoulders.

"Answer the question, darlin'," Seamus demanded.

"Look, not that it's any of your business, but Earl's bark is worse than his bite."

"I don't care. He shouldn't be talking to you that way. I think I'll have a word with him before we leave," Connell stated.

"Are you out of your mind? Are you trying to get me fired?" Leah whispered furiously, tugging against his hold.

"No, Leah, but there is no need for your boss to treat you with such disrespect," Connell replied and let go of her wrist.

"Look, he's just grumpy because I wouldn't go out with him. I'm used to it. Please, I need this job. I don't want you rocking the boat and upsetting Earl any more than he already is. Now, I have work to do, enjoy your burgers," Leah said, turned on her heel, and headed for the kitchen. She could feel their eyes on her as she walked away. It wasn't until she was behind the kitchen door that she relaxed again. She moved toward the pile of dirty dishes and began to scrape and load them into the dishwasher. The sound of Earl's whiney voice grated on her nerves.

"If I catch you fraternizing with the customers again, your fat ass is out of here. I don't pay you to stand around talking all day long."

Leah just rolled her eyes and continued working. She was used to Earl's put-downs, and even though his derogatory comments hurt, she would never let him know that. By the time the dishwasher was on, Earl had finished another order. She took the two plates of food to two of Earl's "best" friends. They were regulars, and they liked to belittle her just as much as Earl did, if not more. She'd learned long ago not to show any emotion. The last thing she wanted was to let the bastards know they upset her.

"Well, if it isn't our fat little cow, Leah," Eli Jones said with a leering grin, his eyes traveling the length of her body.

Leah knew everyone in the diner had heard Eli's comment and felt her cheeks heat once more, this time with humiliation and anger. She glared at Eli and his brother Hershel, but the comments kept rolling around in her head. She had so wanted to pick up his food and dump it in his lap, but she needed this job more than she needed to defend herself, and she knew if she bit back at the nasty men, she would be no better than they were. She turned away from them and caught the O'Hara brothers glaring at the two bastards as she walked back behind the counter.

Leah poured more coffee for the gentlemen sitting at the counter and began to wipe it down. She ignored everyone as she did her chores and dreamed of getting out of the small town of Slick Rock, Colorado, and leaving everything behind.

Leah had grown up in the small town with her mom. They'd lived in a small trailer on the outskirts of town, right on the edge of the national park, ever since she could remember. Her mom had tried to be good to her, but she had been a child herself when she'd had Leah, and even though she'd asked her mom who her father was, her mom had never answered the question.

She didn't think even her mom knew who had created her because she had always just shrugged her shoulders whenever she'd asked. Her mom had slept her way through most of the single men in Slick Rock and even some who weren't single. In fact, her mom had been labeled the town prostitute.

Leah had grown up being shunned and disparaged her whole life and didn't have any friends to speak of. She was treated like her mom had been, as if she would lie down and spread her legs for anything in pants, but that was not the case. She was a good girl, with hopes and dreams of one day leaving all this behind.

Her mom had caught a bad bout of pneumonia two years ago and had never recovered. She passed away six months later, leaving Leah with a stack of bills for a funeral she couldn't afford. She was stuck, and she couldn't see a way out. Every little bit of money she earned left over after paying for expenses went to paying off that debt.

Leah knew she wasn't skinny. She had a full figure with an abundant chest and hips with a small waist in between, but she hadn't thought she was fat until Earl and his buddies had started in on her. Her self-confidence had taken a nosedive, and she had begun to believe she wasn't worthy of a second look. She had worked in this diner since she was eighteen years old, giving her mom whatever she could to help out with the bills. She had been a good girl all her life, and that had gotten her nowhere.

"Hey, Leah, get your fat ass over here and fill my mug," Eli yelled then snickered.

Leah grabbed one of the coffeepots and stormed over to Eli and Hershel's table, she was so tempted to pour the hot coffee over the bastard instead of in his mug, but caught herself just in time. She filled his mug, and as she turned around toward the counter again, she tripped over something. The coffeepot flew out of her hand, shattering on impact. She fell to the floor, her arms outstretched to break her fall, and as her hands the hit the floor, landing amongst glass and hot coffee, they slid over the slick linoleum and she landed on her chest, her forehead bouncing on the floor.

Chapter Two

"She is gorgeous," Seamus said to his brother. "I wish we could take her out of here. Her boss needs a good beating for the way he treats her."

"I know, bro, but we can't interfere beyond giving him a talking to. She's so skittish, she'd run as soon as we looked at her," Connell replied. He and Seamus had both moved further around in the booth so they could watch the beautiful woman as she worked. When he'd heard those two men call Leah fat, it had taken all his self-control not to get up out of his seat and hit the bastards, knocking their teeth into the back of their heads.

Leah was tall for a woman, standing around five foot nine and weighing in around one hundred thirty pounds. She had blonde hair and the saddest brown eyes he'd ever seen. She had a luscious hourglass figure with full breasts and wide hips, just right for a man to hold on to as he loved on her. Connell had felt his cock twitching in his pants and knew by the way his brother shifted in his seat that he was just as affected by her as he was.

Connell could tell by the flush on Leah's cheeks she was humiliated and angry, but she just went about her job, ignoring their verbal jabs. He had wanted to go to her and enfold her in his arms. He had wanted to take away the pain he could see lurking in the depths of her eyes. When he'd heard one of the men yelling at her to get her "fat ass" over to him and give him more coffee, he'd had to grab hold of Seamus's arm to stop him from going over and punching the bastard's lights out. What had happened next had both him and Seamus roaring with fury as they rose to their feet. They didn't get to her in time.

They had been across from her on the other side of the diner, and when he had seen the bastard deliberately trip Leah, sending her sprawling on the floor among hot coffee and shards of glass, his ire snapped.

Connell grabbed the prick by the neck of his T-shirt, lifted him from the chair with one hand, until the man's feet were dangling a foot off the floor, drew back his fist, and plowed it into the man's jaw. He let him go and was satisfied to see he had knocked the man out cold. He turned just in time to see Seamus pick Leah up into his arms and carry her out the front door of the diner. Connell stepped up to the serving window and gave her boss a look which had intimidated many men. He slapped money on the ledge as he stared into the man's eyes and was satisfied when he saw fear looking back at him.

"Leah quits. If I catch you or any of your cohorts near her again, you won't know what hit you," Connell stated in a steely voice. He turned and glared at the other man who had laughed when his brother had tripped Leah and glared. He was pleased to hear the coward whimper. Connell left the diner without a backward glance and headed to Seamus's truck.

"Is she all right?" Connell asked Seamus, who had seated Leah on the edge of the backseat of his truck.

"She's covered in coffee, has cuts on her palms, and has a knot and bruise forming on her forehead," Seamus snarled.

"Well, get her buckled in and we'll take her to see the doctor," Connell replied.

"No. I'm fine, Mr. O'Hara. I need to get back to work," Leah said.

Connell bit back a curse when he heard her voice wobble. No way was she going back in there.

"No, baby girl, you don't. You just quit," Connell replied.

"What? Oh no. You can't. You didn't—What am I going to do now?" Leah asked then burst into tears.

Connell saw the pained look his brother gave him over his shoulder and felt a knot form in his chest. He nudged Seamus aside and scooped Leah up into his arms. He held her while she cried, rocking and soothing her as he inhaled her delicate floral scent and underlying feminine musk. God, she smelled good. He released his hold on her slightly as she pushed against his chest with her small, delicate white hand and looked down into her tearstained face. The sight of the bump and bruise forming on her head had his anger erupting all over again, but he contained it for the benefit of the woman in his arms.

"I have to go back in there. I have bills to pay," Leah wailed.

"Your well-being is more important than money, baby girl," Connell replied. "Besides, we've been looking for someone to cook for us. You can come and work out on our ranch."

"But I don't even know you," Leah replied.

Connell looked down into her sad brown eyes as she looked up at him. The sight of teardrops clinging to blonde eyelashes had his gut clenching. She was so innocent and sweet, he wanted to wrap her up in a warm blanket and keep her there. But he knew that just wasn't possible. Offering her a job on their new cattle ranch was the next best thing, and he intended to see that she took him up on the offer.

"You can check on us with the sheriff if you want to, baby. He'll vouch for us. You have nothing to be scared of with me and Seamus. We would never hurt you. Now, let's get you to the doctor's office, you could still have glass in your skin," Connell explained as he eased Leah onto the backseat of his truck. He helped to swing her legs around and buckled her in. He closed the back door and walked around to the driver's side and slid into the truck just as Seamus got into the front passenger seat.

Connell kept his eye on Leah in the rearview mirror. She looked so sad and alone sitting in the backseat of his truck. He wanted to crawl back there with her and take her into his arms again. It didn't take long for him to drive to the doc's office. He pulled into the lot and got out. Leah was out of the truck before he or Seamus could help her. He took her by the elbow and guided her into the office. He was thankful there was no one in the waiting room.

"Leah needs some attention," Connell said to the receptionist. The elderly woman looked him and Seamus up and down then surprised him by smiling.

"Go on through, Leah, Doc is free."

Leah moved to the inner door, but Connell beat her to it. He held it open and followed her to Doc's inner sanctum.

"Leah, what happened, honey?" the elderly Doc asked as he stood up from behind his desk.

"I had an accident with a coffeepot," Leah replied.

Connell watched as she held up her still-bleeding hands and cussed himself for not wrapping them up. He'd let his anger get a hold and he hadn't been thinking straight.

"Leah didn't have an accident. She was tripped," Connell stated.

"I was not…" Leah began and paused.

Connell could see her thinking back over the incident. Her face was so expressive, he could read every emotion flitting over it.

"What did Earl do? I can't believe he's begun to hurt you physically as well," Doc stated.

"It was Eli," Leah whispered.

"Luke shoulda run those three out of town long ago. We don't like the way Earl and his friends treat you, Leah," Doc said. "Hop on up here and let me take a look."

Connell heard Seamus enter the room but didn't take his eyes off Doc as he examined Leah's hands. The elderly man pulled a large magnifying glass over to her and turned the built-in light on.

"You have a couple of slivers of glass still in there, young lady. Let me get my tweezers and I'll have them out in a flash. You're lucky that you won't need stitches," Doc muttered.

Connell looked on intently as Doc removed the glass, cleaned her hands up with alcohol swabs, placed some gauze over the numerous small cuts, and wrapped her hands up.

"Now, let me see that knot on your forehead," Doc said. "It should be gone in a day or two. Do you have a headache?"

"No, I'm fine," Leah replied.

"I don't want you going back to the diner for a few days, young lady. You need to give your hands time to heal."

"She won't be going back to the diner ever again," Connell stated.

"Well now, I'm glad to hear it. You're Connell and Seamus O'Hara, aren't you?" Doc asked.

"Yes, sir," Connell replied.

"You listen to these two, Leah, they'll take good care of you," Doc stated.

"But…" Leah began.

"No buts, honey. You'll be fine with these two men. They're friends of Luke's. They'll treat you right. Now, change the dressings every day, but don't get them wet. You can take them off in three days. If you have any concerns come back and see me," Doc stated, patting Leah on the shoulder. "We're all done."

"Thanks, Doc," Connell said as he grasped Leah around the waist, helping her to her feet.

"Come on, darlin', let's get you home," Seamus said.

Connell and Seamus each took Leah by the elbows and led her out. She would have gone to the receptionist, but they kept her right on walking until she was outside and in the backseat of the truck.

"But I didn't pay," Leah said in a whisper.

"All taken care of, baby. Now, did you need to collect anything from the diner before we take you home?" Connell asked.

"No, I never take my purse to work, everything I need is in my uniform pockets," Leah replied.

"Good, then let's get you home," Connell stated and gently closed the back door. "We'll need to stop by her place and pick up some clothes. I don't want her feeling uncomfortable, by not having any of her own things at our place."

"She's gonna kick up a fuss," Seamus replied.

"I know, but she doesn't really have a choice. She's going to need our help while her hands are bound up. Come on, let's get this over with," Connell muttered and got into the truck.

"You'll need to direct me to your place, baby," Connell said as he drove out of the doctor's parking lot, glancing in the mirror at her. He saw her cringe and wondered if she was ashamed of where she lived. He kept an eye on her as he drove, and the sight of her nibbling on her bottom lip as she directed him made his cock jerk in his pants. He could just imagine what she would look like with her beautiful pink lips wrapped around his dick as she knelt before him, and he nearly groaned out loud. She was the sexiest, sweetest woman he'd ever laid eyes on, and he knew Seamus felt the same way. He and Seamus had both been looking for a woman to share since they had retired from the Marines.

Connell and Seamus had always been attracted to the same women. When their friend Luke Sun-Walker had told him about his own ménage relationship and the others forming in the small rural town in Colorado, he and his brother had been intrigued. They had talked it over and decided that they also wanted to have a ménage relationship. And when they had finished serving their time for their country, they had decided to relocate as well.

They had been in Slick Rock for just over six months and had been so busy setting up their new cattle ranch they hadn't taken the time out to see any of the females in the small Colorado town. They had been to the diner a couple of times, but had never seen Leah there before. She must have had days off both times he and Seamus had eaten at the diner. Pity, they could have saved her from six months of hell. He knew Leah was the woman for them and now they were going to take the time to get to know her and try and ease her into a ménage relationship.

Connell kept his face blank when he saw the old trailer standing in the middle of a nowhere. He saw no car and wondered if Leah had left it at the diner, but then remembered she said she'd left nothing behind.

"How do you get to and from work every day, Leah?" Connell asked, as he turned the truck off.

"I walk," Leah replied. "Thank you for bringing me home."

"No problem, darlin'. Why don't you give me your keys and I'll get the door?" Seamus asked.

Connell got out and saw his brother open the back door, helping Leah out of the truck.

"You don't have to see me in, I'll be fine," Leah said, moving toward the dilapidated trailer.

"Yes, we do, darlin', you need some help to pack up your things," Seamus said.

Connell saw Leah freeze, her hand halting on the key she'd just pushed into the lock. She turned her head and looked over her shoulder at him then Seamus.

"What? What do you mean?"

"You're coming home with us, baby. I thought I'd already told you we were hiring you to come and cook for us," Connell stated.

"But—but I don't even know you."

"What's to know? You need a job and we need a cook. I am thirty-five years old, an ex-Marine, and just started a cattle ranch with Seamus," Connell said.

"I'm thirty-three, retired from the Marines eight months ago, and can't cook worth a damn," Seamus stated.

"Come on, Leah, you don't have a job anymore and we need a cook. You're going to need our help until your hands have healed. So what do you say, baby? Are you going to come and put us out of our misery and cook for us once your hands are better?" Connell asked.

Connell watched as Leah nibbled on her bottom lip again. It was obviously a habit she had taken to when she was nervous or concentrating real hard. He wanted to pull her to his mouth and soothe the hurt she was inflicting on herself, but knew it was way too soon to make a move on her. He wanted her feeling comfortable around him and Seamus before they began to try and woo her into their hearts and beds. He knew as soon as he saw her staring up at him and his brother like a doe caught in headlights that she was the woman they had been waiting for. Now all they had to do was convince her she wanted them just as much.

Chapter Three

Leah glanced up to see Connell watching her in the mirror. She felt her cheeks heat again and lowered her eyes. His gaze had been hot enough to singe her with its fire. She wondered if she was crazy as Connell drove, heading to their ranch with her in the backseat. The thought of actually living on their ranch and having a large, spacious room of her own for the first time in her life, rather than the cramped confines of a trailer, was just too good to pass up.

She hadn't put up much of a fuss, and she wondered if she'd taken leave of her senses, letting them talk her into packing up her stuff and going with them. There was just something about the two large men that got under her skin. She'd thought she had enough of pining over men when she'd had a crush on the new sheriff, Damon Osborn, and had felt a little hurt when he and his brothers had hooked up with their new fiancée, Rachel Lamb. It had taken the two handsome men walking into the diner for her to realize she had only been interested in the sheriff. He hadn't made her body stand up and take notice the way it did with the two O'Hara brothers. And the sound of their lyrical Irish accents just made her shiver and her pussy weep.

Leah turned her head and looked out the side window. She wondered what her mom would think about her jumping at the opportunity of having her own room instead of living in a rundown trailer on the edge of the national parkland. Even though her mother had been promiscuous, Leah knew her mom had done it because she was lonely and for the gifts she had received from her men. She had often pawned those gifts for money which had helped to keep a roof over their heads, food in their bellies, and clothes on their backs.

She'd also raised Leah to be a good girl, drumming morals into her she hadn't practiced herself. Her mother had had to drop out of school at the age of fifteen when she found out she was pregnant and her own parents had kicked her to the gutter. Leah had no idea who her grandparents were and didn't even know if they were still alive. As far as she was concerned, after the way they had treated her mother, they could rot in hell.

Leah closed her eyes as she leaned her now-aching head on the cool glass window. She wondered if she'd done the right thing or if she was making a huge mistake. Only time would tell, and if things didn't work out she could always go back to her mom's trailer. What she'd do for work if that happened, she had no idea.

The sound of the truck slowing had her lifting her head and opening her eyes. She looked around and couldn't help her breath halting in her chest when she saw the new ranch house, barn, stables, and other outbuildings. She'd heard through the grapevine that Earl's parents had had to sell up or foreclose to the bank and knew Earl had moved to the apartment over the diner, but she'd had no idea who had bought the property, until now. She looked around in awe, seeing nothing of the old house that used to be here. She'd come out to this place with her mom once and still, to this day, had no idea why her mom had come here. All she knew was that her mom and Earl's parents had argued over something, and when they had left, her mother was upset, with tears in her eyes. Her mom had never brought her back again.

Everything was so new and clean. Even the corral near the barn was made from fresh timber. She stared at the large, long ranch house with the new timber decking and breathed out. *What the hell am I doing? I don't belong here.*

Leah looked around as she got out of the truck. Seamus held the door and helped her down by holding her elbow. She could see the beginnings of a vegetable garden near the side of the house and the bare beds of a flower garden running the length of the timber deck.

She turned back to the truck and went to grab one of her bags from the backseat, but to her surprise, she was lifted out of the way.

"No you don't, darlin'. You'll hurt your hands," Seamus stated.

Leah was even more surprised when he held her by the waist until she was steady on her feet, then reached in and grabbed her two bags.

"Come on in, baby girl, and let's get you settled," Connell said.

Leah walked to the steps of the decking and hesitated. She felt as if her whole life was about to change and there was nothing she could do to stop it. She took a deep breath, placed her foot onto the first step, and kept right on going. She didn't have much of a choice at the moment, but she would save every penny she earned, and when she had enough money to leave, she was heading out on the first bus out of Slick Rock, regardless of where it was traveling to. She followed Connell as he led her into the house and the next stage of her miserable life.

Leah looked around her, and she followed Connell through the mudroom into a hallway. The hall had several doorways leading off it and then widened out into the biggest living room she'd ever seen. She saw a huge television up on the wall and noted the furniture wasn't small and delicate, but large and chunky, no doubt a good fit for the large men who owned it.

"This is the living room as you can see. The kitchen and dining room are through there," Connell said, pointing his finger for her benefit. "If you'll follow me, baby, I'll show you to your room."

Leah followed Connell, peeking in open doorways as they passed. He led her to the end of the hallway off the living room and opened a door to the left. He walked in and put the small bag she had directed them to pack for her, containing some of her mother's precious belongings, onto the bed. He walked over to a closet and showed her where she could hang her clothes. The bed in the room was huge compared to the single bed she'd slept on in the kitchen area of the trailer. The bed was covered in a maroon quilt with matching covered pillows. The closet was bigger than the small bathroom in the trailer, and she knew her pitiful amount of clothes would look lost in the large space.

"There is a bathroom down the hall, baby, second door on your left. The first door is Seamus's room and the one next to yours at the end of the hallway is my room. You'll find towels in the cupboard on the right in the hall and there are more in the one in the bathroom. If you need anything all you have to do is holler. All right?" Connell asked.

Leah was so overwhelmed by Connell and Seamus's generosity and the sheer size of everything that she couldn't answer. She gave a nod of her head as she took in the chest of drawers against the wall next to the doorway and the timber dresser beside it. Her clothes wouldn't even fill the drawers. She felt tears pricking the back of her eyeballs and turned away, hoping Connell hadn't seen them. She kept her head lowered and saw boots standing beside her.

"You okay, darlin'?" Seamus asked.

Leah blinked a few times, dispelling the moisture from her eyes and looked up to see Seamus looking at her with concern. She gave him a tremulous smile, nodded her head, and lowered it once more. She saw Seamus place her bags on the bed, and then he lifted her head to his with a gentle fist beneath her chin. She hadn't even heard him enter the room. How such a big man could move without making any noise was beyond her comprehension.

"Why don't I run you a bath and you can have a soak while I put your clothes away?" Seamus asked.

"That would be nice, thank you. But you don't need to put my clothes away. I can do it later."

"We know you can, baby, but Seamus wants to. You're going to need help with your bath, Leah. Doc told you to keep the bandages dry." Connell's lyrical voice rumbled through her as he moved in close to her back.

"I'll manage," Leah replied. "It's only my palms that got cut, not my fingers."

"Okay, but if you need any help, all you have to do is call out," Connell said as he placed his hands on her shoulders and turned her to face him. "Why don't you sit down on the bed, baby? You're looking a bit worn out. Do you have a headache?"

"Yes, just a bit of one."

"I'll get you some painkillers and a glass of water," Connell said.

Leah sank down onto the side of the bed. Connell left for her painkillers, and Seamus left to run her a bath. She could hear the tub filling and couldn't wait to soak away her aches. Her body was sore from her fall, and she knew a hot bath was just what she needed to help ease her pain. Connell was back moment later, and he handed her two pills and a glass of water. He watched over her as she downed the tablets and then handed the glass back.

"Thank you."

"You're welcome, baby. Go take your bath and when you're done, have a nap. That will help get rid of your headache."

"Your bath is ready, darlin'. Go and have a good soak, but call out if you need any help," Seamus said as he looked at her from the bedroom door.

Leah unzipped one of her bags, ignoring the sting the actions caused the palms of her hands, and gathered up some clothes. She skirted around Connell and slid past Seamus as he moved back. She scurried to the bathroom and closed the door behind her. She had no trouble getting out of her coffee-stained pink uniform, but her bra was a different matter. She won in the end, determined not to have to call for help and have the two men see her fat body clad only in her underwear. The last thing she wanted was for them to see her high-waist granny panties and plain white cotton bra. She never had the money to splurge on pretty underwear and had always bemoaned the fact she had only ever bought the serviceable cotton variety. Not that she should care. No one was ever going to see it, anyway.

Leah moaned with delight as she slid into the bathtub, the hot water enveloping her tired, aching muscles. Her body had begun to stiffen up from her fall, her knees were aching, and her cut hands were beginning to throb. She rested her arms along the rim of the tub and realized she wasn't going to be able to wash herself. Luckily Seamus had poured some fragrant oil into the bathwater, so she wouldn't smell nasty at least, and the water was rinsing away any sweat and grime she may have accumulated since she began her shift at six that morning. She heard heavy footsteps coming toward the bathroom and held her breath as they stopped outside the closed door. A light knock had her jerking upright in the tub, her sudden movement sloshing water over the rim.

"Are you all right, baby? Do you need any help?" Connell's voice asked through the closed door.

"No. I'm fine, thanks."

"Okay, but don't hesitate to yell out if you need any help, Leah. You don't need to be embarrassed. I promise to keep my eyes to myself."

"I–I'm good," Leah replied hesitantly, then slumped with relief as she heard his footsteps taking him away from the bathroom door.

She wasn't good at all, but she was too ashamed of her heavy breasts, wide hips, and plump thighs. She never looked at herself in a mirror and would die of embarrassment if anyone else saw her fat, dimpled ass. The pain in her head had diminished to a dull ache. The painkillers had taken the edge off and her hands were sore from the numerous cuts, but as long as she didn't try to use them too much, the pain was bearable.

Leah leaned her head back against the rim of the tub and closed her eyes. She had nowhere else to go now she was no longer working at the diner. She wasn't worried about losing the job. She had hated working with Earl and putting up with his nasty comments as well as his friends, but she'd had to have money to live and working at the diner had become a habit. She had learned to ignore Earl's snide remarks about her body, just putting out her hand for her small paycheck each week. Even her mom had tried to get her to look for work elsewhere, but Earl had done a real job on her self-confidence. And wasn't it better to stay with the devil you knew than to go to the devil you didn't?

Leah sighed as her body began to relax and didn't even realize she was in danger of falling asleep in the tub until it was too late. She slid down under the water and came up sputtering and coughing. She used her hands and gripped the rim of the tubs so tightly she felt her healing flesh split open again. Her hair was in her eyes, covering her face, and she was still spluttering, trying to clear the water from her lungs. The door slammed open, and one set of hands reached for her before she could protest. She was lifted from the tub as if she weighed nothing, and another set wrapped her up in a large towel, and then she was sitting on hard, muscular thighs, her hair being pushed back away from her face.

"Are you all right, darlin'? What happened?" Seamus asked.

"I fell asleep," Leah replied and lowered her eyes. She was so aware of the taut thighs rippling beneath her ass, and she could feel her pussy creaming.

"You've got your bandages wet and your hands are bleeding again. Why don't you let us help you dry off and get dressed, and then I'll change the dressing on your hands?" Connell's voice came from above her head.

She couldn't prevent the shiver her body gave as the deep timbre of his voice rumbled against her shoulder and vibrated through her body down to her core, making her pussy quake even more. She thought it over and knew since they had probably already seen her body and she was in no shape to do things for herself, she was going to have to relent and let them help her this time.

"Do you promise not to gawk?" she asked and cursed the fact her voice wavered.

"We promise, darlin'," Seamus replied. "Come on, stand up and we'll get you dried off."

Leah held still and kept her eyes on theirs as they dried her off. She could see Connell's eyes in the mirror and on the wall opposite her as he gently dried her now-wet, tangled hair. He'd already removed the elastic from around her hair and let it fall down her back. They were both good to their word and kept their eyes on hers until they had her dried and dressed. Connell picked up a brush off the bathroom counter and pulled it through her hair, systematically removing all the knots until her wet hair hung down to the top of her ass. She knew, before the day was over, once it was dry again, it would be back to its wavy, uncontrollable state.

Leah had never felt so pampered in her life. She'd only ever had her mom brush her hair, and that was as a child. She couldn't remember the last time someone had taken the time to give her a hug or an encouraging word. Her mom had always been too busy with her lovers, and she had always spent her time working to get money and gifts from her men.

She lowered her eyes as tears pricked them. She didn't want to the two men to see how their kind attention and care affected her.

Chapter Four

"Relax, baby, I've got you."

Connell had seen the sheen of tears in her eyes after he had finished brushing Leah's hair. He wondered how long it had been since anyone had taken the time to give her a hug. He could see the emotional starvation in the depths of her gaze and wanted to take that look away. He wanted to curl her up in his arms and hold her tight. He also wanted to bury his cock so far into the depths of her luscious body that he could feel the head of his erection butting against her cervix, but he knew she wasn't ready for that yet. He slid an arm around her shoulders and the other down beneath her knees and lifted her into his arms. Her shriek of surprise had him biting back a grin. She wrapped her arms around his neck and clung to him tight.

"I'm too heavy, Connell, put me down."

"No, I won't drop you, Leah. You don't even weigh half as much as I do, baby. There's not much to you at all. I'm just taking you out to the kitchen. The light is better out there and I can redo the dressing on your hands. Why didn't you call out for help?" Connell asked, looking down into her face as he carried her out of the bathroom and down the hallway.

"I was fine until I fell asleep. I must have slipped under the water and by the time I got my breath back you and Seamus were already there to help me," Leah replied.

Connell sat down in one of the kitchen chairs and pulled her down with him. He knew she must have been able to feel his hard cock pressing against her hip, but she didn't move to get away from it, for which he was grateful. He knew if she was wriggling around on his lap he would be in danger of coming in his own pants, and he hadn't done that for over fifteen years, when he was still a wet-behind-the-ears, green lad having erotic dreams.

Connell gently placed her hands on to the tabletop and began to unwrap her bandaged limbs. He could see fresh blood seeping out onto the surface of the wet, white gauze. Seamus came and sat down next to him and Leah, placing the large first-aid kit on the table. Seamus picked up her other hand and began to remove the soiled bandage. Connell disinfected and rewrapped one hand while Seamus did the same with the other.

"There you go, baby, all clean and dry," Connell said and placed a kiss on her temple. "Would you like a drink? How is your head? Are your hands hurting too badly?"

"My head is fine now, thank you. My hands are stinging like a bitch and I would kill for a coffee," Leah replied. Then she surprised him by leaning her head back on his shoulder and sighing contentedly.

"I'll get your coffee, darlin'. How do you have it?" Seamus asked.

"White, no sugar, please."

"You're all worn out, aren't you, baby? Why don't we go into the living room and you can put your feet up for a while?" Connell asked, but didn't wait for an answer. He was already lifting her into his arms and striding toward the door.

"I can walk, you know. My legs aren't affected at all," Leah stated, then gave a nervous giggle.

"I know you can, Leah, but I love the feel of you in my arms. Just relax and enjoy being pampered for a change, baby. Here we are," Connell said as he eased her down on to the large leather sofa. He sat down beside her, picked her legs up, and pulled them onto his lap. He began to massage her bare feet as she sat with her back in the corner of the sofa, and he loved the feel of her warm, soft flesh beneath his fingers.

"Here ya go, darlin'," Seamus said.

* * * *

Leah watched as he pulled the coffee table closer to the sofa and put her cup down on it. She couldn't believe how tender and caring these two men were being toward her. She'd never had that before, not since she was a small child. She reached out for the mug of coffee, but Connell's big hand beat her to it. He handed the mug to her and waited until she gave a nod indicating she had a good grip on the cup and let go. From the corner of her eye she saw Seamus sit down in the large armchair next to her.

"How long have you been working at the diner, Leah?" Seamus asked.

"Four years," she replied.

"Has your boss always treated you so badly?" Connell asked.

"Yeah, pretty much, but he's been worse in the last six months or so."

"Why do you put up with it, darlin'?" asked Seamus.

"I have bills to pay, just like everyone else. If I don't earn money the bills don't get paid," Leah answered and cursed mentally when she heard her own voice tremble. She saw Seamus give Connell a look, and then they both turned back to her.

"What bills, baby?" Connell asked quietly.

"My mom's funeral expenses," Leah said, a hitch in her breathing. "My mom did the best she could, but we never had much money. There was no money for luxuries and there was no way she could afford life insurance."

"So you've been working all the hours you could, taking abuse from that bastard to pay off a debt?" Connell asked.

Leah was too choked up at his quiet understanding to reply. Her chest and throat felt so tight, like she had a huge lump stuck there, and she was having trouble breathing, so she gave a nod of her head. She closed her eyes as she felt the tears well and knew she wasn't going to be able to keep them at bay this time. She felt the first tears trickle down her cheeks and tried to turn her face away so the two men sitting close to her couldn't see. But she knew she'd failed when she felt Connell move his arm beneath her leg, the other around her waist, and he pulled her onto his lap. She hid her face against his chest and gave in to the emotion choking her. Not once did Connell try and get her to stop crying. He held her tight and rocked her as she sobbed. When her emotional storm finally subsided, she wiped her tears away with the back of her bandaged hands and looked up into Connell's eyes.

"I'm sorry. I don't usually cry. I don't know what's gotten into me," Leah said.

"Hey, don't be apologizing, baby. You've had to be so strong for so long, it was inevitable you would feel so much emotion when you were shown a bit of human kindness," Connell replied.

"Aren't I keeping you from your work? You don't have to babysit me, you know," Leah said.

"I know that, baby. We have a few ranch hands to take over when need be, so don't you worry over us spending time with you, instead of working. We will get back to work tomorrow, but since the day's almost done, I didn't see much point in heading back out."

"Well, thank you for taking the time to look after me. I really appreciate it," Leah said and snuggled back into Connell's embrace. She felt a large bulge forming beneath her hip and knew Connell was becoming aroused. She tried to sit up again, intending to get off his lap, but Connell wouldn't let her. He held her firmly against him, but didn't hurt her. The sound and feel of his deep, lyrical voice rumbling against her side and face made her pussy ache with need. She didn't know she could ever feel so horny just by the sound of a male's voice until she'd met Connell and Seamus. Her sexuality was just beginning to awaken, and she didn't know what to do about it.

"Just relax, Leah. I promise I'll never hurt you, baby," Connell whispered against her ear.

Leah couldn't prevent herself from squirming as a shiver raced up her spine. His warm, moist breath on the skin of her ear was turning her on even more. Her nipples hardened into tight little points, and her pussy clenched, releasing more of her cream.

"Look at me, Leah," Connell demanded.

Leah sat up straight on Connell's lap and looked into his eyes. What she saw in the gray depths made her clit throb and her pussy contract as waves of desire hit her. He was looking at her with such heat in his eyes she felt the singe down to her bones.

"I can smell you creaming for me, baby. Let me make you feel good."

Leah was shocked to hear Connell talking about what she had just been thinking and opened her mouth to speak. The words never left her mouth. Connell smothered her mouth with his own, sliding his lips across hers, and his tongue slipped in between her lips and rubbed against hers. She couldn't help but respond in kind. She opened her mouth wider for him and hesitantly moved her tongue along his. She shivered when she heard a growl erupting from his mouth into hers and had the air leaving her lungs. She felt him tip her body back onto his muscular arm, supporting her weight as his fingers tangled through her still-damp hair. His large hand held her head to his as he devoured her mouth.

Leah whimpered as Connell's free hand glided beneath her top, his fingers and the palm of his hand roaming over her sensitive skin. His hand was so large he practically covered her whole abdomen as he splayed his fingers. She cried out with desire as she felt the tips of his fingers rub the underside of her bra-clad breasts and arched her upper body into his touch. She'd never felt anything so pleasurable in her life, and he hadn't even touched her intimately yet.

Leah bowed and whimpered when Connell's hand enveloped her breast. His large hand engulfing all of her flesh made her blood boil. He shaped and kneaded her with his hand and fingers, and then he rubbed the tip of his thumb back and forth over her hard nipple through the cotton fabric of her bra. The pleasure was so exquisite. She wanted more. She mewled into his mouth when she felt him pinch her nipple between his finger and thumb. She arched her hips up, seeking the relief her body craved. She felt another hand at the waistband of her jeans, pulling open the button and sliding down the zipper.

She tilted her head back as Connell's mouth withdrew from hers and kissed his way across her jaw to her ear, giving him easier access to her neck. She cried out when he nipped at her earlobe. He licked and nibbled down the side of her throat until he came to the place where her shoulder and neck joined. He scraped his teeth over the sensitive skin, and she pushed her hips up with the pleasure.

Leah felt her jeans and panties being pulled down over her thighs, calves, and feet. She thought about protesting, but that thought faded away as Connell took her mouth beneath his once more. The taste of his tongue on hers was an aphrodisiac in itself, one she couldn't get enough of. She wrapped her hand around the back of his neck, holding his head to hers, exploring every nook and cranny with her own tongue.

* * * *

Seamus stared at the bare pink mound revealed to him as he pulled Leah's jeans and panties off. She was so pretty and sexy. The sight of her lush, plump, dew-covered folds was more than he could stand. He gently pried her thighs apart by running his hands up the inside of her silky, soft white skin, leaned over her, and inhaled deeply. The aroma of musky, feminine arousal made his cock push against the zipper in his jeans, and he had to adjust himself to a more comfortable position. She was so sexy with her body aroused because of him and his brother. Her cheeks had a rosy hue, and her drying blonde hair was spilling down around her shoulders and over the arm of the sofa. The sounds she made as he and Connell pleasured her only made him more determined to hear her scream with rapture.

Seamus licked through her wet folds with the tip of his tongue. Gathering her juices as he went, he groaned at the clean, fresh taste of feminine cream as he swallowed her essence down. He placed his hands on her hips and made himself more comfortable, using his shoulders to spread her legs even farther apart. He flattened his tongue and licked over the sensitive, engorged bundle of nerves peeking out from the top of her slit. He twirled and lapped over her clit and gripped her more firmly as she writhed beneath him. He opened his eyes, and the sight of her luscious breasts, now naked to his gaze, made his balls ache along with his cock. His brother was sucking on the tip of one tit as he pinched the other with his free hand. He lapped at her clit, faster and harder, even more turned on by the incredible sounds emitting from her throat.

Seamus placed one of his hands on top of her pubic bone, his thumb resting in the top crease of her pussy, and pulled the skin up, releasing her little pink clit from its small hood. He bent his head back down, licked and nibbled on that little pearl of flesh until she was sobbing incoherently with pleasure. He used a finger on his other hand and rimmed around the edge of her cunt hole, coating the end of his digit with her cream. He eased the tip into her flesh and moaned as her muscles clamped down on him. His little minx was trying to draw his finger farther into her body. He lapped at her clit and slowly pushed his digit deeper into her hot, tight, wet sheath. He slowly began to pump his finger in and out of her cunt as he flicked his tongue over her now-protruding clit. He felt her walls tighten and ripple around his digit and knew she was close to climax. He thrust his finger faster and deeper, making sure to slide the pad of his finger over her sweet spot.

Seamus heard her long, low scream as her cunt clamped down and she bucked beneath his hands and mouth. He kept thrusting his finger in and out of her contracting pussy, making sure to give her every bit of pleasure as she climaxed. He slurped up her juices as they gushed from her body. He and Connell soothed her down from her climatic high by rubbing her skin with light, easy touches until her breathing slowed once more.

"Oh. My. God. I can't believe I let you do that," Leah said as she sat up, crossing her arms over her chest and one leg over the other.

"What's not to believe, darlin'? You were horny and in need. We wanted to pleasure you," Seamus replied.

"But, I've never done anything like that before. I'm just as bad as my mother was."

"What do you mean by that, baby?" Connell asked, taking her chin in his hand, turning her head to meet his gaze.

"My mother was the town whore. Looks like the apple never falls far from the tree."

"Don't ever let me hear you say that again, Leah. You're not your mother. Just because you let us give you a climax, let us make you feel good, doesn't mean you're a whore," Connell said firmly but quietly.

"Are you still a virgin, darlin'?" Seamus asked.

"Well, I was but I don't suppose I am anymore," Leah replied.

"You are still a virgin, darlin' and there is no way in hell you're a whore." Seamus reiterated his brother's words. "Most women have had at least two lovers by the time they're your age and we wouldn't label them whores either."

"Really?"

"Yes really. Come on, let us help you get dressed and then we'll make some supper," Seamus said. "I'm hungry."

Chapter Five

Leah set the timer on the oven and sighed. Her hands had healed nicely, and over the next couple of weeks she got into a routine of cleaning house and cooking meals for the O'Hara brothers. They hadn't made any more moves on her since her first night in their home, and she wondered if the sight of her fat, naked body had turned them off. But then she would catch them watching her with such heat in their eyes she wondered how her hair hadn't been singed from her head. They took the opportunity to touch her often, on the arms, the back, and even gave her a pat on the ass. Both of them always gave her a peck on the lips and a hug each morning and evening. She felt like she was a sexual time bomb with all their teasing touches and found at times she had to physically restrain herself from jumping their bones.

Leah had just finished the last preparation for supper and put the casserole in the oven when the phone rang.

"Hello."

"You don't deserve to be living with those two men in their house. You need to die, you fat bitch."

Leah's hand shook as she replaced the receiver. She felt cold to the bones, but sweat broke out on her forehead. The voice had definitely been a male's, but whoever it was had disguised their voice in a low, fierce whisper. She wondered if her ex-boss had found out where she was, or maybe one of his dumbass friends. She had no idea what she'd done to deserve that call, those threatening words, and hoped she never found out.

She heard horse hooves pounding into the ground, rushed over to the window, and looked out. The sight of Connell and Seamus riding horses bigger than they were, their legs gripping their mounts' sides, made her cream her panties. They were such big, rugged men. The muscles in their thighs rippling as they rode, as well as the sinew and striations in the forearms moving as they controlled their mounts, turned her on every time she saw them. She watched as they dismounted and handed the reins of their horses over to one of the ranch hands then turned toward the house.

Leah was in the process of setting the table with utensils, plates, dinner rolls, and butter as they entered the mudroom. She heard their boots hit the floor, and then she knew they would head for showers to clean up before dinner. She looked up when she heard the rustle of clothes and gazed into Connell's stormy gray eyes.

"What's wrong, baby?" Connell asked.

"Nothing, dinner is nearly ready and should be hot by the time you've cleaned up," Leah replied, her eyes moving away from his.

"Are you lying to me, Leah?" Connell asked, and moved farther into the room.

"No."

"Look at me when you talk to me, baby," Connell stated. He reached out and took her chin between his fingers and thumb. "Now answer the question again. What's wrong?"

"I got a phone call a few minutes ago," Leah explained.

"And?" Connell asked.

"It wasn't very nice."

"Who was it? What did they say?"

"They said I didn't deserve to be living here with you in your house and that I needed to die."

"What the fuck? Who would do such a thing?" Seamus roared.

Leah turned toward the door where Seamus was standing, his stance aggressive. His hips were thrust forward, his hands were on his hips, and she could see anger radiating from his eyes. She hadn't even known he was there until he spoke.

"Connell, call Luke and Damon, I want them putting a tap on the phone line," Seamus said.

"I don't think that's really necessary, Seamus. It was probably just some kid dialing random numbers getting kicks," Leah said.

"You don't believe that any more than we do, do you, baby?" Connell asked. "I think it's time you and I paid Earl a little visit, Seamus."

"You can't do that, Connell. You don't have any proof it was Earl or his toadies," Leah said.

"Fuck, Leah's right. I'll call Luke and get him or Damon to put a trace on our line. There's nothing we can do until we've got proof," Seamus stated.

"Why don't you two go clean up? Dinner will be on the table by the time you're done," Leah said, turning toward the kitchen.

"Don't let that bastard get to you, baby. He's not worth it," Connell said from behind her.

Leah sighed as Connell wrapped his arms around her waist and drew her back against his front. She felt him kiss her head as he gave her a squeeze and released her once more. She loved that they hugged, touched, and kissed her all the time. The only thing that worried her about it was that she was beginning to have feelings for the two big men. She was scared of getting her heart broken in two.

As they ate dinner Leah listened to Connell and Seamus discussing what needed to be done on their ranch. She didn't listen to their actual conversation, but the deep timbre of Connell's voice and Seamus's gravelly, lyrical cadence made her squirm in her seat. She didn't know what it was about the two men that turned her on so much, but she didn't care. They were so loving and protective of her, and she lapped up every bit of their attention. She knew she had been starved of human companionship from an early age and hoped the two big men didn't see her attention as too desperate. Not that they'd ever said anything, and they were the ones touching and kissing her. So maybe she was reading more into it than she should. She was so confused. Why hadn't they tried to make another move toward her since that wonderful first night? Maybe the sight of her body had turned them off after all, and they were just too polite to say anything.

Leah pushed her half-eaten meal aside and drank her glass of water. Whenever her mind was in tumult her appetite always seemed to suffer.

"What's wrong, darlin'? Why aren't you eating your food?" Seamus asked.

Leah looked up and gave a shrug of her shoulders. "I'm just not that hungry, I guess."

"You look tired, baby. Why don't you let Seamus and I clean up the kitchen and go and have a soak in the tub?" Connell suggested.

"I can't let you two clean up in here. You've been working hard all day," Leah protested.

"Yeah, you can. I insist. You're looking a little pale, baby. I don't want you getting sick. Now, go on and have a bath. We'll clean up the dishes," Connell reiterated.

Leah sighed, gave them a nod, and left for her bath.

* * * *

"What do you think is worrying her?" Seamus asked.

"I don't know. She's been a little down the last couple of days, so it wasn't just that phone call."

"She is so sexy. Every time I see her or just think about her I get hard enough to pound nails," Seamus groaned out.

"Yeah, me, too," Connell stated. "Do you think it's too early to make our next move on her?"

"Nah. She looks at you like she's starving. She wriggles and squirms in her seat and her nipples get hard," Seamus told his brother.

"She looks at you the same way, whenever she thinks we're not watching her. I think it's time we make love to her and make her ours. I feel I've got a case of blue balls after holding back for so long," Connell explained. "Let's get this mess cleaned up and see if she'll accept us loving on her together."

Chapter Six

Leah had her eyes closed and her head resting on a rolled-up towel on the edge of the bathtub. She heard a faint click but was too tired to lift her head and open her eyes. The odor of her favorite scent, frangipani, floated up to her from the warm water, and she inhaled the wonderful, relaxing fragrance. An unfamiliar noise penetrated her senses, and she opened her eyes to see Connell and Seamus standing before her, gloriously nude.

"So, are you going to join me, or are you just going to stand there staring?"

She felt her areolas pucker and her nipples go hard as she stared with openmouthed stupefaction. The two men were so packed full of muscle their arms rested inches from the sides of their bodies. They each had hair on their chests. Seamus's was a light mixture of blonde and light brown between his pectoral muscles, and she couldn't stop her eyes from following that treasure trail down to the prize. His cock was huge and erect. The head of his cock was level with his belly button, and it moved slightly with every beat of his heart.

Leah slid her eyes over to Connell. He had a dark thatch of hair framing his cock, and he was even more impressive than his brother. His cock was so wide and long she squeezed her legs together in nervous anticipation. She let her eyes travel up the length of Connell's body, taking in the rippling of his abs and pecs as he shifted on his feet. She met his eyes and felt her blood heat, her pussy soften and weep, and knew she was in trouble. She now knew that the two men standing before her wanted her as much as she wanted them, and there was no way in hell she was turning them away. She'd been waiting for this moment ever since she had first laid eyes on them. Leah nearly laughed when both the men scrambled to get into the tub.

Connell sat down on her left, and Seamus sat to her right.

"Do you have any idea how gorgeous you are, darlin'?" Seamus said, leaning over and down until his face was inches from hers.

"Really? You truly think I'm pretty?" Leah asked, noting the breathless quality of her own voice.

"Nah, darlin', you're not pretty. You are the sexiest, most beautiful woman I've ever laid eyes on. You have me hard just by breathing," Seamus said.

Leah reached up with her hands, wrapped her arms around his neck, and pulled his mouth down the last couple of inches. He slid his moist, warm lips over hers, and she gave herself over to him. She opened her mouth as he swept his tongue inside, and she reciprocated by tangling her tongue along his. His tongue twirled and explored every crevice, and he nibbled on her bottom lip. When the need for air intruded Seamus pulled back away from her, and she was happy to hear him breathing just as heavily as she was.

"My turn," Connell rasped out.

Leah turned her head at the sound of Connell's voice and saw him nudge Seamus out of his way. She felt his hands at her waist, and then she was being pulled onto his lap. She ended up straddling his thighs, her ass resting on his firm quads and her breasts mashed against his hard chest. She looked up at him to find his head was already lowering to hers. He consumed her mouth, taking her body, heart, and soul along for the ride. She knew in that moment that she was going to get hurt, but she was going to take every bit of love and affection the two brothers gave her until it was over. At least then she would have the memories to look back on and know she had felt love for two very special men.

Leah moaned into Connell's mouth as his tongue moved over hers. She couldn't get enough of his taste. He was such a big man she felt so small and feminine in his arms, surrounded by his warmth. She felt a slick hand roaming over her and the heat of Seamus's body at her back. He slid his hands between her and Connell's chests as he began to lather her breast with bodywash. She pulled her mouth from Connell's, her breathing fast, and leaned her back against Seamus's chest. She cried out as he pinched her nipples, which made her arch up, begging for more.

"Stand up, darlin'," Seamus demanded in a deep, raspy voice. "I want to wash your sexy body."

Leah stood and was thankful for Seamus's steady arm. He wrapped one large, muscular arm around her waist to help her to her feet and to keep her from slipping. She saw Seamus pass the bottle of bodywash over to Connell, and he squirted some of the thick, yellow, viscous fluid into the palm of his hand. Then she moaned and leaned back into Seamus as four hands glided over every inch of her naked skin, washing her from head to toe. Once they were done, Connell tugged her down and he and Seamus rinsed her off.

She clutched at Connell's shoulders when he scooped her up into his arms, and he carried her out of the tub. Seamus was already waiting with a large bath towel, and when his brother set her on her feet, Seamus began to dry her off. He was quick and efficient with his movements but very gentle with her. The two men then concentrated on drying themselves so quickly she couldn't prevent a gurgle of laughter from escaping her mouth.

"You should do that more often, baby," Connell said.

"What?"

"Laugh," Connell answered. "When you laugh it lights up your whole face and you have the cutest little dimple which peeks out, right here. Come on, let's get you to bed. You're dead on your feet."

Connell picked Leah up and carried her through to the bedroom. He placed her into the middle of the bed and got in beside her. She felt the mattress dip, and then Seamus's front was plastered against the length of her back. Connell pulled her into his big body with an arm around her shoulders, giving her his bicep to use as a pillow, his front facing her. She felt hands caressing up and down her back, over her hips and stomach. Then Connell pulled her thigh up over one of his hips and slid his hand down to her mound. He rimmed a large finger around her pussy hole, gathered some of her juices, and glided back up through her wet folds. He rubbed the pad of his finger over her clit and had her back up to flash point in seconds.

Leah moaned and bucked her hips as her belly grew heavy with liquid heat. She was on fire, and only the two men with her could put out the flames. She felt Seamus slide his hands up her rib cage and cup her breasts. He pinched and pulled on her nipples, making electric pulses travel straight down to her cunt. She could feel her cream leaking from her pussy onto her thigh and wanted one of them to make love to her now. She whimpered as Connell eased the tip of another finger into her pussy and began to massage her clit with his thumb. She couldn't get enough. She rocked her hips, trying to get his finger deeper into her wet sheath, to relieve the throbbing ache inside her. She opened her eyes to see Connell staring down at her, a grimace of pleasure on his face as he watched her. She reached up and brought his mouth down to hers, opened up to him, and kissed him with abandon.

Leah felt Connell slide his finger further into her depths and couldn't stop her flinch of pain as he stretched her hymen. She'd heard it could be painful to have sex for the first time, but it also depended on the woman. Connell withdrew his mouth from hers and looked deeply into her eyes.

"Baby, are you sure you want to do this? We haven't even discussed about us wanting to share you," Connell stated.

"Why do you want to love me together?"

"Seamus and I have always been interested in the same women. When we were younger we started thinking about sharing a woman, but we didn't think any woman would be interested, so we never pursued the idea. Luke Sun-Walker is a friend of ours, and he told us of his unique relationship as well as the others in this town. We decided that is the sort of relationship we wanted as well and here we are," Connell explained.

"I'm attracted to you both and as much as I want this I'm afraid of causing trouble between you. The last thing I want to do is make either of you jealous and affect the relationship you have with each other."

"Darlin', that will never happen. We want to make love to you together and yes, sometimes separately as well. But we will never be jealous of you spending time with each of us. We trust each other implicitly and we know you would never play one of us off against the other," Seamus elucidated.

"You don't know that I wouldn't. You hardly know me."

"Yes we do, baby. You are the sweetest, kindest person we have ever met. Now, are you still sure you want this? Do you still want us to make love with you?" Connell asked again.

"Yes, I'm sure. I want, no, need you to make love to me. Both of you," Leah replied.

"If we do this, Leah, you will be ours. There'll be no going back. Do understand, baby?" Connell asked.

Leah looked at Connell and wondered if he meant for this moment or until their relationship died a natural death. Because she knew it was inevitable that this would not last. She wanted, needed, to experience their love, so she gave a nod of her head in reply.

Connell shifted and moved her onto her back. He kissed her lightly on the lips and worked his way down her body. He licked and nibbled on her neck, down to her breasts where he took one of her sensitive nipples between his lips and teeth. He sucked and scraped that sensitive little peak until she was writhing beneath him with pleasure. She cried out as Seamus took her other nipple into his mouth, and she wondered if a person could die from too much pleasure.

Connell moved down her body, nipping and sliding his tongue over the sensitive skin of her belly. She felt him kiss the top of her mound as he used his broad shoulders to spread her legs wide. The first lick of his tongue from her clit to her ass was so good she bucked her hips up into his mouth. She felt him wrap his arm around her upper thighs, and he tilted her hips up more. She was totally exposed to him and wondered why she didn't feel vulnerable. She realized it was because she loved them. She relaxed back on the pillow and gave her body over to their care.

Leah moaned as Connell laved on her clit with the tip of his tongue, and she felt him begin to penetrate her cunt with his finger once more. She was beside herself as pleasure consumed her body and senses. He eased that finger in and out of her body, going deeper with every push. She flinched when she felt his digit stretch the thin membrane of skin inside and then moaned as he sucked her clit into his mouth. He held her clit lightly between his teeth and flicked the tip of his tongue over the distended nub.

She could feel liquid seeping out of her pussy, and the muscles in her womb, belly, and vagina began to coil tight. She knew what was happening but couldn't prevent her mind from fighting against the pleasure. Seamus must have seen her reaction because he removed his mouth from the tip of her breast and began to speak soothingly into her ear.

"Don't fight it, darlin'. Let go. We only want to make you feel good. Let Connell fuck you with his mouth. You are gonna fly so high. Let go, Leah. We'll catch you," Seamus crooned.

Leah thrashed her head from side to side on the pillow. Her body was trembling because she was coiled so tight. She arched her neck and wailed with pleasure as the muscles in her cunt snapped down hard on the finger buried to the hilt in her pussy. Not once did Connell let up from laving her clit until the last ripple and spasm had died.

Connell lifted his head and looked up the length of her body until she met his eyes. She could see the juices from her pussy glistening on his mouth and chin. She watched as Connell wiped the moisture from his face and licked his fingers clean.

"You taste so good, baby. I could spend hours eating your sexy little cunt," Connell stated.

Chapter Seven

Connell crawled up over Leah's supine body and leaned down to kiss her. The knowledge that he was sharing the taste of cunt made his cock bounce and his balls ache. He wanted to bury himself in her hot, tight, wet sheath and pound on her until they were both screaming, but he knew he was going to have to be gentle with her. She'd never been with a man before, and he didn't want to hurt her. The thought of being her first had him wanting to pound on his chest and declare his own masculinity, but he knew that wasn't an option. He had never felt possessive of a woman before, but Leah seemed to bring that primitive side of him to the surface.

He braced himself on his arms as he withdrew his mouth from hers and was glad to see the return of desire in her eyes when she opened them to look up at him. He held her gaze with his as he reached over to the bedside table and withdrew a small foil pack. He tore it open with his teeth and rolled the condom over his erection. He slid a hand beneath her ass, grasped her fleshy buttock in his large palm, and tilted her hips up. He nudged the head of his cock into her hole and groaned as her wet, hot flesh enveloped the head of his rod tighter than his own fist would. Yeah, he was definitely going to take it slow and easy. He was a big man everywhere, and the last thing he wanted was to cause Leah pain.

Connell held still until she became accustomed to his size and penetration, and he knew she was ready for more when she stopped clenching on him. He eased in more and moaned as her wet warmth surrounded him. He slid back and then moved forward again, gaining more depth with every slow pump of his hips. It was pure heaven to be wrapped in such a tight glove, and hell, too, because he wanted to surge in until his balls were flush with her ass. He took a few deep breaths, tightening the leash on his body's control, and began to move a little faster and deeper. He bit the inside of his cheek as he felt her cunt grab at his hard dick and then release him once more. He looked up to see Seamus move his head to her tits and suck one of her hard nipples into his mouth. He pumped his hips back and forth until finally he felt his balls touch her ass. She was so tight he was in danger of shooting off way too early.

Connell moved his hand to the top of her mound again, and began to strum over her clit. He flicked gently and began to surge in and out of her cunt. The wet slurping sounds as his cock slid in and out of her juices only seemed to enhance his desire. When he felt her legs and belly begin to tremble he knew she was close to orgasm. He pumped his hips, sliding his cock in and out of her pussy, pushing down on her clit a little firmer as he massaged the little button faster and faster. He knew he was out of control now, and he couldn't have stopped if his life depended on it. The sound of his and Leah's flesh slapping together only added to the carnality of their lovemaking. He saw her face go slack with pleasure, her mouth open as she panted for air, and she shoved her hips back up at him, meeting his every thrust. He was glad to see he wasn't hurting her and that she seemed to be with him every step of the way.

Leah screamed as her cunt muscles gripped him so tight he could have sworn she was going to break his cock in half. The sensation of her muscles gripping and releasing as the walls of her pussy rippled along his dick was enough to take him with her. He felt the tingles at the base of his spine travel around to his crotch. His balls drew up tight to his body, and then he was shooting deep into her cunt. He roared as her body milked every last drop from his balls and cock. He felt the prophylactic covering his dick catch his semen, and then he collapsed down on her. He used his elbows to keep most of his weight from her, not wanting to crush her or hurt her in any way. He gave her a slow, easy kiss and smiled as he noted her glazed-over eyes. He eased his now semierect cock from her pussy, careful not to pull out too fast. He stroked his hand over her belly and headed for the bathroom to clean up.

* * * *

"How are you feeling, darlin'?" Seamus asked.

"I feel good," Leah answered and gave him a smile.

"Do you think you're up for some more lovin'?"

Leah didn't answer him. Instead she reached up and brought his mouth down to hers. He growled as he thrust his tongue into her mouth. He swept it all over, exploring and finding all her secret pleasures. He was lost. He knew he would never get enough of the loving, sexy woman in his arms. He wanted to keep her by his side and in his bed forever. He wanted to be able to love and protect her for the rest of his life.

Seamus eased his mouth from hers and nibbled down her neck. When he reached her breasts he suckled on one nipple and pinched the other between his thumb and finger. She responded so well to his touch. She arched her breasts up into his mouth and hand, and he felt her rub her wet pussy onto one of his thighs. It seemed Leah was more than ready for some more loving. He released her nipple with a loud pop and then made his way down her body until he reached her mound. He wrapped his arms around her thighs and spread her wide as he tilted her hips up and pushed her knees back toward her chest.

The sight of her flushed, wet labia had him groaning out loud, and he bent his head to taste her. He shoved the tip of his tongue into the wet little hole and used one of his thumbs to lightly rub on her clit. He felt her internal muscles ripple around the tip of his tongue, and she coated his muscle with more of her juices. He lapped and licked, making sure not to waste a single drop of her cream. When he heard her sobbing breaths escalate and her body began to tremble, he knew

Leah was on the verge of climax. He withdrew his mouth and sat up between her thighs, reached for a condom, and sheathed his cock. He slid his crotch up close to her, fisted the base of his cock, and aimed for her sweet, wet hole.

Seamus growled as he watched the head of his cock disappear into Leah's snatch. It was one of the hottest sights he'd ever seen. He continued to lightly massage her clit, rubbing in circles getting smaller and tighter as he slowly pushed his hard rod into her depths. He stopped when he was buried balls-deep, giving her time to adjust to having his erection in her body. He felt her ripple along the length of his shaft, grasped her pelvis, and began to pump his hips.

He had never born such pleasure before, and he felt as if they were connected on a higher level as his cock slid in and out of her cunt. He believed he could see into the depths of her soul and knew she didn't realize he could see the love she felt for him shining from her eyes. He kept his gaze glued to hers and began to love her with everything he had.

Seamus noticed that Connell had reentered the room and was lying on the bed. He had been so wrapped up in Leah he hadn't even seen his brother return. He looked over and saw his brother felt the same as he did. There was no way in hell they were ever letting this special, loving woman get away from them. She was theirs, and no one else was going to get the chance to have her.

Seamus let his control off the tight leash he'd had it on and began to love her in earnest. The sensation of his balls slapping on her ass as he thrust his cock in and out of her wet sheath was nearly more than he could stand. He was in danger of losing his wad way too early. He thrust in and out of her, harder, faster, and deeper. The sounds she made as he loved on her had his spine tingling and his balls drawing up tight. He reached between their bodies, took her clit between his finger and thumb, and gently pinched.

Leah screamed and arched her hips up into him as her pussy walls clamped down on his hard rod. The feel of her squeezing and releasing on his hard shaft was enough to take him over the edge with her. He plunged one last time, held himself still as he pulled her hips up to him, and yelled with pleasure as he spewed his load into the end of the condom. When the last shudder and convulsion had died, he eased his cock from her tight, dripping hole, being careful to take the condom with him. He flopped down beside her, still breathing heavily as he tried to will strength back into his shaking limbs. He'd never had a woman affect him the way Leah did and knew he was in love for the first time. He looked over at Connell and knew by the look on his brother's face he felt the same way.

Chapter Eight

Leah checked the stew she had cooking and let her mind drift. She had never felt so loved and appreciated. She spent her days taking care of the house, doing the laundry, and cooking meals for her men. And her nights she spent in the arms of the two O'Hara brothers. They were so protective of her, and she soaked up the love and attention. She began to learn to love the shape of her body all over again. Connell and Seamus were always complimenting her, telling how sexy she was and what a delight her body and her uninhibited responses to them were. The weeks passed by so quickly it wasn't long before the long, hot summer began to die and the nights became cooler and the days shorter. There hadn't been any more of those dreaded phone calls, and she began to relax, believing it had just been a kid mucking around making random calls.

Leah had just pulled the big pot of stew off the stove when she heard the sound of horses' hooves pounding the earth, as she did every night. She hurried out the back door, eager to catch a glimpse of her men and their sexy bodies swaying with the movement of their mounts. It seemed she couldn't get enough of watching her men and made sure she went out to the wood deck every night to greet them. Just as she reached the timber rail and leaned her hands on the top she heard the sound of a car coming up the long gravel drive.

Leah turned her head to see who their visitor was and saw a gleaming black sports car pull up close to the barn. She watched with curiosity as a small, svelte woman dressed in designer-label clothes got out of the car and headed toward the barn where her men had disappeared. Curiosity got the better of her, and Leah moved from the deck and down the steps. She stopped just outside the open doors of the barn when she heard the woman talking.

"Please can you forgive me? Connell, Seamus, I'm sorry for not keeping in contact with you. It was just such a shock to find out you both wanted to share me. I now know I was scared of what I was feeling and that I love you both more than anything."

Leah didn't hang around to hear the rest. She felt pain pierce her heart and had to concentrate on not doubling over with the agony. She knew she should have been warier when she had arrived here. But the two men had worked their way beneath her skin and into her heart so quickly her head was still spinning. She had to get out of here. *God, what am I going to do? I don't have a job and the trailer is five miles away. How the hell am I going to get all my stuff back home? Look on the bright side, Leah, at least you'll be able to check up on your real home.*

Leah hurried inside to her room and packed up her stuff, not bothering with folding anything. She just threw everything into her bags and zipped them up. She went to the kitchen and called a cab. She grabbed the two small bags, crept out the front door, and took off down the drive. There was no way she could compete in the looks department with such a small, good-looking, sophisticated woman and had no intention of even trying. Leah made sure to keep off to the edge of the drive, knowing the trees along the length would keep her hidden from view. By the time she got to the gate a taxi was just pulling up. She got into the back and didn't look behind once.

* * * *

Leah hadn't felt well since she had arrived back home. She shifted on the double bed in the small trailer her mom had once occupied and felt every muscle in her body ache as she did. She knew she was getting sick and probably should go see Doc, but she didn't have the energy to call for a cab, and there was no way she could walk the distance in her current state. She had spent the night crying her eyes out and had hardly slept. She had felt as if her body was on fire, yet she was shivering because she was cold. Her cell phone had rung on and off throughout the night, and when she'd seen the screen displaying Connell's and Seamus's names she switched it off. She must be a glutton for punishment because not two hours later she had turned her phone back on. The sight of a restricted phone number displayed had piqued her curiosity, and she had answered. She wished she hadn't now, but hindsight was a wonderful thing.

The echo of that low, disguised voice had sent shivers of fear racing up and down her spine.

"I told you, you aren't good enough to be living with those men. You are such a slut. You need to die."

Leah had no idea who would want to hurt her, and even less an idea of why. But she was too sick at the moment to care. She saw light peeking through the gap in the curtains and closed her eyes for the first time since she'd left Connell and Seamus.

* * * *

"Why the fuck would she leave us, Connell? I know she loved us, I could see it in her eyes," Seamus yelled with frustration.

"I don't know. I would have thought she would have come to us if she had a problem. She has before. Fuck it. I can't stand this. I can't believe she would just up and leave without telling us or leaving a note. She won't even answer her phone." Connell roared with hurt fury. "It's too late to do anything now, but first thing in the morning we go looking for her. If she doesn't want to come back then that's her decision, but I am not leaving until I have an explanation."

Connell watched Seamus move to the bar in the far corner of the living room. His brother poured two glasses of whiskey neat and handed one to him. Connell wanted to get in his truck and go searching for Leah but knew he and his brother needed to calm down before they confronted her. They didn't want to alienate her any more than it seemed they already had. He still had no idea why she'd left, but he had a huge knot in his gut which wouldn't let up and knew he and Seamus were somehow the reason for her leaving. He felt sick to his stomach as he thought back over everything he and Seamus had done and said. He couldn't come up with one reason why Leah would leave them.

"Connell, did you think to look to see if Leah was waiting for us on the porch like she normally does when we ride into the yard?"

"No. I was too shocked to see Debbie's car driving up as we rode into the barn."

"That's it. Don't you see? Leah would have seen Debbie and maybe the sight of her sent her confidence to rock bottom again. Think about it. What would a woman who had been verbally abused and belittled about her size feel when she saw someone like Debbie? What if she heard what Debbie was saying to us and didn't hang around to hear what we said in reply? Fuck. She's gonna be hurting so bad. We have to get to her and explain, Connell," Seamus said.

"Yeah, you're right, let's go and find her now. We both know where she's gone. Now that we know what may have sent her running we can go and ask her about it," Connell stated and downed his whiskey in one gulp. He relished the slow burn the whiskey gave him as it warmed his insides. The knot in his gut let go for the first time since he had found Leah was missing. He pulled his keys from his pocket and was about to head out, but his cell ringing stopped him. Their ranch foreman had just let him know about one of the mares having trouble with birthing. They were going to have to wait until morning before they went after Leah. He sighed with frustration and headed out to the barn, Seamus on his heels.

Once he and Seamus explained to Leah and she was back in their arms, he was never letting her leave again. If he had his way she would marry him as soon as he could arrange it.

Chapter Nine

Leah moaned and coughed as she rolled to her side. Her whole body was on fire, and yet she was shivering so hard her teeth were chattering. She sniffed through a clogged nose and caught the hint of smoke in the air. She wondered who was setting a fire and drifted in and out of consciousness. She was so tired and she knew she should be getting up, but for some reason had no idea why. She heard shouting outside and raised her hands to cover her ears. The noise was making her skull ache, and she couldn't stand the pain it caused to her head. She felt around for her pillow and pulled it over her head.

She felt arms wrap around her and sighed as she snuggled into a familiar hard chest. A car door slammed closed, and she tried to open her eyes, but it was too much effort. When she surfaced again she was in a tub of cold water. She thrashed, pushing at hands as she tried to get them to stop torturing her. She was so cold and tired she wanted to wrap herself in a blanket and sleep for days on end. She heard deep voices as she drifted but couldn't make out what they were saying. Everything sounded so garbled, and she was too tired to try and work it out. How long she drifted in that surreal world she had no idea, and for some reason she didn't seem to care.

When she surfaced again she thought someone was trying to drown her. Firm hands were holding her head and shoulders up, and they were trying to get her to drink. The cool liquid trickling into her mouth triggered her thirst, and she gulped down the thirst-quenching water. She screamed with fury as the glass was taken from her before she was finished. *Why are they torturing me this way?*

She was being moved again. *Why can't they leave me alone and let me die in peace?* Leah heard a scream from far away as her cold body was plunged into even colder water again. *Why are they being so cruel to me? What have I done to deserve this type of treatment?* Her throat was so sore and dry she felt as if she could drink a whole barrel full of water.

Leah was in bed again. It seemed she had just taken a sip of water, not enough to quench her thirst, and it was being taken away again. She opened her mouth to scream, but nothing more than a raspy sound came out, and she drifted back to sleep.

She fought the hands pulling at her clothes, wanting them to leave her alone so she could sleep. She was so tired, and her whole body was one big ache. She tried to yell at them to leave her alone, but either they couldn't hear her or they just ignored her. They pulled her this way and that, and then she was being placed back onto the bed, the covers were pulled back over her, and she sighed as she drifted back to sleep.

Leah woke up and moaned as her aching muscles protested. She felt as if she'd been in a car wreck and couldn't work out why she felt so bad. She opened her eyes, blinking a few times as her eyes adjusted to the light. She felt so sweaty and dirty she wanted to have a shower, but didn't know if she had the energy to get up. She looked around and knew she was back in her room at Connell and Seamus's ranch. She wondered how she'd gotten back here because the last thing she remembered was leaving in a cab. She tried to push herself up, but her arms were so weak they wouldn't cooperate. Then she remembered she had actually made it back home, and she knew she was sick. She'd heard there was a new strain of influenza making the rounds and wondered if that was what she'd caught. The sound of footsteps walking toward her room had her eyes glued to the door. She watched warily as Connell and Seamus entered the room.

"Baby, how are you feeling?" Connell asked.

"Terrible," Leah replied. The sound of her own voice was so low and raspy Leah knew she must have been pretty sick.

"You're looking much better, darlin'," Seamus stated.

"How did I get here?" Leah asked.

She watched as Connell and Seamus moved farther into the room and took a seat on either side of the bed.

"We brought you here, baby. Why did you leave us, Leah? If you had any concerns you could have come and talked them through with us. Why did you leave without saying good-bye or leaving a note?" Connell asked.

Leah could see she had hurt him and Seamus deeply. It was there in their eyes, but they had hurt her just as much.

"That woman," Leah began and licked her dry lips. She saw Connell get up, and he poured her a glass of water from the jug on the bedside table. He handed her the glass, and she drank thirstily. She placed the glass back on the bedside and turned back to Connell.

"That woman said she loved you," Leah said.

"Yes, she did, and did you hang around to ask us about her or to hear what our reply was? You couldn't have, otherwise you wouldn't have left. Debbie is in our past, baby. We hadn't seen or heard from Debbie for nearly twelve months. We thought we were in love with her and wanted to have a ménage relationship with her. She was too shocked and scared to try. And I thank God every day that she left. She wasn't the one we needed. We were in love with the idea of sharing her, not actually in love with her. We didn't even realize that until we met you. You showed us what real love was, baby. I love you so much and want to spend the rest of my life with you, Leah," Connell said quietly.

Leah felt tears trickle from the corners of her eyes, and she turned to look at Seamus.

"I love you, too, darlin'. Please give us a chance to show you we really do love you, Leah. You mean the world to us and I can't bear the thought of not having you by my side," Seamus declared.

Leah's throat was now sorer than before, after talking earlier so she didn't try to speak, and she was too weak to throw herself into their arms. So she lifted her hand and beckoned them to her with the crook of a finger. The two men enveloped her in their warm embraces. She inhaled their familiar scents and knew she was where she was supposed to be. She'd saved herself for these two men and was mighty glad she had. They were a weakness she never wanted to get over. They were her one and true plunge into love, and she intended to relish every moment she was in their arms.

"I love you, too," Leah rasped and squeaked when the four arms around her hugged her tight. They moved away slightly and eased her back down onto the bed. She could feel her eyelids beginning to close already and knew she was falling asleep again. But this time she had a smile on her face as she drifted off.

* * * *

Leah found out she had been so sick that her men had called in Doc to examine her. Her temperature had raged for three long days, and her men had taken turns looking after her. They had submerged her in icy baths, kept her fluids up, changed her sweat-soaked shirts, and changed the bed linen. She had wondered why they had looked as bad as she felt, and the knowledge that they had nursed her, taken care of her while she was so sick only made her love them more.

On the fifth day she was well enough to get out of bed for the first time. She looked around for her clothes, and when she couldn't find any, grabbed the clean T-shirt draped over a chair and headed to the bathroom. She showered and savored feeling clean after washing her hair and body. She pulled the T-shirt on and wrapped herself in one of the large robes hanging on the back of the door and went in search of her two men.

Leah found Connell and Seamus in the kitchen drinking coffee. She headed to the pot, but Seamus ushered her over to a seat at the table and took over the task for her.

"You're looking a lot better, baby," Connell said.

"I feel much better. I'm sorry you had to look after me," Leah stated.

"I'm not. We love you, Leah. We wanted to take care of you while you were sick."

"Well, thank you. Both of you. I just hope neither of you ends up sick because you took care of me," Leah said.

"If we do, then there is nothing we can do about it, darlin'. We'll just ride it out the same as you did," Seamus replied.

"Still, I hope you don't. That was one nasty bug. Where are my clothes?" Leah asked. "I looked but couldn't find them."

"Leah, don't you remember the fire?" Connell asked with a frown.

"Fire? What fire?"

"When we came to the trailer to get you, darlin', the trailer was on fire. We got you out and away from it just before the gas bottle exploded and engulfed the trailer in flames," Seamus enunciated.

"Oh no, all of my mom's things were in there. All my clothes, my purse, my cell phone, they're all gone. Shit. What am I going to do now?" Leah sobbed.

Leah felt arms around her waist and looked up as Seamus pulled her onto his lap, enfolding her in his arms.

"I'm sorry, darlin'. We would have tried to save your things, but it was too dangerous. We only just got you out in time," Seamus explained, and she heard a tremble in his voice as he remembered what she never would. "I thank God that we arrived when we did."

"I had another one of those calls. Whoever it is had my cell number," Leah said and shuddered.

"What did they say, baby?" Connell asked.

"Um," Leah said as she thought back to that call. "It's hard to remember, but something like I wasn't good enough to be with you. That I was a slut for living with you both and I needed to die."

"I'll call and let Luke know. We need to keep an eye out in case someone is after you. I trust my gut and I don't like what my intuition is telling me," Connell said.

Leah looked up to Connell and asked the question she didn't really want to hear the answer to, but she was better off knowing than remaining ignorant.

"What's your gut telling you, Connell?"

"That you're in danger, baby. I think you're being stalked."

Chapter Ten

Leah checked the cornbread she had put into the oven. She was glad to be back home where she belonged. She felt so much better about their relationship now that Connell had explained to her about Debbie. She was still worried about who could be out to get her, but she pushed that thought to the back of her mind. There was nothing she could do about it at the moment. Her two men had been sleeping with her every night since she had gotten over that dreaded flu bug, but they hadn't tried to love her. She was becoming sexually frustrated now that she knew what she was missing out on. She knew Connell and Seamus were giving her body time to heal, but she was well now and needed them more than ever. She was determined to get them to love her tonight. After all, it had been two weeks.

Leah had prepared a baked dinner since the weather was cool enough and had just removed the beef from the oven, transferred it to a platter, and covered it to rest when she heard her men galloping into the yard. She rushed outside and stood on the porch watching as they slowed their mounts to a walk. She'd put on one of the new dresses her men had bought for her and stood waiting to greet them. A sharp crack echoed through the air, and she spun around to look behind her. Of course there was no one there. She felt intense pain in her arm, but ignored it as her men came running from the barn.

She had no idea what was wrong, but they looked furious and they were barreling toward her as fast as they could. She ran to meet them and squeaked in surprise when Seamus tackled her to the ground. He rolled as they landed so he took the brunt of their landing, but she still felt the air whoosh from her lungs. She moaned with pain as her upper arm connected with the hard ground.

"Are you all right, darlin'?" Seamus's voice whispered in her ear.

"Yes, I'm fine. What are we doing on the ground?"

"Someone tried to shoot you, Leah. Didn't you hear the shot?"

"Shit, I thought it was a car backfiring."

"Are you hurt anywhere?"

"Just my arm, it hit the ground when you tackled me."

"I'm going to roll you over to take a look, but keep your head down. I don't know if whoever tried to shoot you is still around. Okay?"

"Okay," Leah replied. "Where's Connell? Connell, where are you?"

"I'm okay, baby. Just stay with Seamus and let him take care of you. I'll be back in a bit," Connell replied.

Leah tried to lift her head to see Connell, but Seamus used a hand and pushed against her forehead.

"Keep that head down, darlin'. Connell will be fine. We're trained Marines, remember? Now, let me see that arm," Seamus said and moved slightly to the right.

"Fuck, Leah. You've been shot."

"What? Where?" Leah asked, trying to see as she craned her neck sideways.

"Stay still, darlin'. I need you to stay calm for me, all right?" Seamus asked.

"I'm fine, Seamus. I promise, but my arm is hurting like a bitch."

"I don't doubt that it is. You're lucky it's just a graze. God, when I heard that shot, my heart stopped. I need to get you inside so we can call in Luke and Damon, but I think you should see Doc first," Seamus said.

"Can't you just fix it?" Leah asked.

"No, Leah. You're going to need antibiotic ointment on the graze so it doesn't get infected."

"Seamus?" Leah said, her voice sounding weak even to her.

"Yeah, darlin'?"

"I don't feel very well," Leah whispered. She felt the blood drain from her face. Her eyeballs roll back in her head, and passed out.

* * * *

Seamus looked up to see Connell heading back from behind the barn. He shook his head, letting him know there was no sign of the shooter, and saw his brother look at Leah. The sight of her pale face and her closed eyes had his brother's eyes wandering her body. They snagged on the blood dripping from her upper arm, and the tortured sound emitting from Connell's mouth echoed his own turmoil.

"It's just a graze, Connell, there's no bullet in her arm. Go and call Doc and then get both the sheriffs out here," Seamus said as he moved off Leah and gently picked her up. He carried her into the house and down to her bedroom. Connell followed behind, his cell phone to his ear.

Seamus gently placed Leah on the bed and rushed to the bathroom for a towel. He wrapped it around her arm, pulling it tight to stop her blood from flowing. He sat down next to her, feeling useless as he and Connell waited for Doc and the sheriffs to arrive. He smoothed her hair back from her face and smiled at her when she opened her eyes.

"Are you okay, darlin'?" Seamus asked, knowing he'd already asked her that question before. But he needed to hear her sweet voice letting him know she was still here with them. The thought of someone shooting at her had rage building up inside him, and he wanted to get up, go find who had shot her, and kill them with his bare hands. He breathed in and out a few times, trying to control his fury, and relaxed at the sound of his woman answering.

"Of course I'm all right. I just had a little nap and feel like I could take on the world," Leah replied.

Seamus knew then that she was going to be all right. The fact that she was trying to put him at ease with humor when she had to be in a lot of pain had him smiling again. She was such a strong, feisty little thing when she wanted to be. He knew she fit with him and Connell as if she had been made specifically for them.

Seamus looked up at Connell when he heard two cars on the gravel drive close to the house and knew the two sheriffs and Doc had arrived. Connell left the room to let them in. Seamus gave a nod to Doc as he entered the room and moved to the end of the bed to give the elderly man room to work.

"Hi, Leah, what have you done to yourself?" Doc asked.

"Well, I didn't do it, but someone took a shot at me," Leah replied.

Seamus saw Doc flinch at her nonchalant statement and shook his head. The elderly man sighed, but then he got down to work. He had Leah's wound cleaned up and wrapped in no time. Doc left the room after giving Leah and him instructions on her care, and Seamus rushed to her side when she sat up.

"Where do you think you're going? Doc told you to rest."

"I'm going to the bathroom and when I'm done I'm going to the kitchen for a cup of coffee. I'm fine, Seamus, I promise," Leah reiterated.

Seamus nuzzled her hand as she placed her palm onto his cheek. He kissed her on the forehead and headed to the kitchen.

"Seamus," Sheriff Luke Sun-Walker greeted him as he entered the kitchen.

"Luke, Damon," Seamus replied as he shook the two sheriffs' hands.

"Did you see anyone?" Luke asked.

"No. I was too hell-bent on getting to Leah so whoever the motherfucker was couldn't take another easy shot at her," Seamus replied. "Have you been watching Earl and his cohorts?"

"Yes, when we could, but there are only the two of us, Seamus, and we can't be everywhere at once," Luke replied. "I don't think Earl and his friends have enough backbone to do something like this."

"Have you looked for the slug yet?" Seamus asked.

"No. We'll do that as soon as we've talked to Leah," Luke replied.

"You called?" Leah asked.

Seamus jumped to his feet at the sound of her voice, took hold of her elbow, and steered her to the table. He pulled her down onto his lap and wrapped his arms around her.

"Hey, I wanted coffee," Leah stated.

"I'll get your coffee, baby. You just sit and rest," Connell said.

"Leah, did you see anyone when you were outside?" Luke asked.

"No. I went out onto the veranda like I usually do when Connell and Seamus come home, and I was watching them," Leah replied, her cheeks pinkening with heat.

"Did you hear the gunshot, Leah?" Sheriff Damon Osborn asked.

Leah nodded and explained the details of the incident.

"Hm, okay. Well, I think I'll go see if I can find the slug. Good to see you so happy, Leah," Damon said with a wink.

Seamus wondered what that was about and intended to find out later, but for now he was comforted by the feel of her on his lap and in his arms, safe and sound. Leah picked up her mug of coffee, and he noticed her hand was shaking. He knew what that meant. She was suffering from an adrenaline crash and would be shaking all over in a minute. He took the cup from her hand and placed it on the table.

"Connell, go get Leah a shot of whiskey," Seamus commanded.

"B–But I–I don't even like whi–whiskey," Leah said through chattering teeth.

"Darlin', you're suffering from an adrenaline crash. The whiskey will help you get your equilibrium back. It'll warm you up quick and you'll feel much better. Okay?" Seamus said then kissed her on the temple.

He looked up when Damon entered the room again. He had a slug in a small plastic bag, and Seamus knew his friend would run it through ballistics and for prints.

Seamus let Connell see Luke and Damon to the door. He wasn't letting Leah out of his sight, not after some asshole had tried to shoot her. He wanted to take her to the bedroom and lose himself in her body, her scent, the feel of her skin beneath his hands and mouth. He wanted to bury his cock in her pussy, the reaffirmation of life after a near-death experience. But he knew he couldn't do that to her. She was probably in too much pain. He hugged her to him, leaned down, and licked her neck. The sound of her moaning made his cock go from resting to hard in two seconds flat.

She turned in his arms until she was sitting on his lap sideways. She took his face between her hands and looked deeply into his eyes.

"I love you, Seamus," she whispered.

"I love you, too, darlin'," he replied.

"Will you please make love to me? I need you."

"Leah, I want that more than you could ever know, but you've just been shot. I don't want to hurt your arm," Seamus replied.

"I know you'll be careful of me, Seamus. I trust you. Please?"

Seamus didn't reply this time. He just scooped her up in his arms and headed to the bedroom.

Chapter Eleven

Seamus let Leah's feet touch the floor. He kept his hands on her waist until she was steady on her feet and began to help her disrobe. He walked up behind her, slid the zipper of her dress down, and helped her ease the dress off her arms and down to pool at her feet. He held her steady again as she stepped out of the material then helped her to sit on the side of the bed. He bent down, picked up one of her feet, and removed her shoe, then did the same to the other foot. He slid the palms of his hands up her calves to her knees and then up over her thighs.

"Are you sure about this, darlin'? The last thing I want is to hurt you," Seamus stated.

"I'm sure. I love you so much and I'm very horny."

Seamus smiled and knew Leah also needed to reconnect physically after such a traumatic experience. He reached up behind her, unhooked her bra, carefully slid the straps over her injury, and then pulled it off. The sight of her full, heavy breasts with their dusky, coral tips had his cock aching, and he couldn't stop himself from taking a taste. He leaned forward and licked across one nipple then gave the other the same treatment. He sat back and watched her areolas pucker as the cool air touched on the now-wet peaks. He looked up to see Leah gazing down at him with enough heat in her eyes to make his blood boil.

Seamus reached for the waistband of her panties and pulled them from under her ass, down over her thighs and calves, and off. The sight of her newly shaven, nude mound had him growling in the back of his throat. He stood up, picked her up, and placed her in the middle of the bed, then began to remove his own clothes. He climbed onto the bed when he was naked, covered her body with his own, and took her mouth beneath his.

Seamus slid his lips over hers, gently at first, savoring the contact of her lips against his own. He built the heat slowly, sweeping his hands down her sides, loving the feel of her warm, soft, silky skin under his palms. He licked across her lower lip then thrust his tongue into her moist cavern and entwined it with hers. He moved to his knees on the bed, taking her with him, pulling her up so she was sitting on her ass, her breasts brushing his chest. He leaned back and took in the sight of her rosy cheeks, her passion-glazed eyes, and her swollen lips. Her hair was tumbling down her back, and she had never looked so sexy. He took her in his arms once more and helped her to lie back on the bed. He kissed and licked his way down her luscious body, paying attention to both her nipples, then slid his tongue down her stomach and rimmed her navel.

Seamus knew he'd found another of her erogenous zones when she bucked her hips up at him. He swirled and dipped his tongue into the small indentation and then slid his tongue down her lower abdomen until his mouth hovered over her mound. He stared at her bare pussy in awe as he inhaled her delectable, musky, feminine scent. The sight of her dew-coated lips and her engorged clit peeking out at him had his passion unleashing. He moved until he was lying comfortably between her legs, smoothed the palms of his hands up her inner thighs, and spread her limbs wide.

Seamus dipped his head down as he used his thumbs to gently part her plump labia and took his first taste. He slid his tongue from the top of her slit down to her cunt, dipped his tongue into her creamy hole, and continued down to her ass. He licked over the sensitive puckered flesh of her anus then stiffened his tongue and pushed in.

"Seamus, what are you doing?" Leah asked breathlessly.

"I'm loving you, darlin'. Does what I did feel nice?"

"Yes."

"Then just relax and let me make you feel good. Nothing we do in the bedroom is wrong, Leah, as long as we are all consenting. If you don't like what Connell or I do, all you have to do is say no. Okay, darlin'?"

"Okay," Leah replied.

Seamus licked his way back up to her clit and flicked over the sensitive little nub with his tongue. He rimmed her cunt hole with a finger and slowly pushed in. The feel of her clamping down on him had his balls aching, and he knew he had to bury his cock in her body soon. But for now he wanted to love on her and just relish the feel of her body beneath his hands and mouth. He pumped in and out of her, making sure to slide the pad of his finger over her G-spot, and growled with approval when she coated his finger and hand with more of her juices.

He kept his tongue working over her sweet little clit, withdrew his finger, and massaged her cream into the skin of her asshole. He collected more of her liquid and took it back down to her sweet little pucker. He felt the muscles in her ass relax and pushed the tip of his finger into her dark entrance. The sound of her scream as he sent her over the edge into bliss with the tip of his finger wiggling in her ass and his tongue rubbing on her clit was music to his ears.

"Leah, are you all right?" Connell's anxious voice had Seamus looking up and over his shoulder.

"Don't answer that, baby. I can see you're fine," Connell said.

"She's more than fine. She's fucking hot," Seamus replied and saw his brother move to the side of the bed and start removing his clothes.

Seamus lowered his head once more and flicked the tip of his tongue over her clit. He withdrew his finger from her ass, collected more of her cream, and moved his digits back down to her anus. He pushed two fingers into her back door, easing them through her tight sphincter until he was in as far as he could go. He spread his fingers and began to thrust them in and out of her canal. The sounds Leah made only made him more determined to send her screaming over the edge into nirvana once more. He slid his third finger into her cunt and pumped in and out of her pussy and ass. He nibbled and sucked on her clit all the while he massaged her internal nerves. He opened his eyes and looked up over her delectable body to see Connell sucking on one of her nipples while pinching the other between his thumb and finger.

Seamus felt her pussy and ass squeeze down on his fingers and knew Leah was about to explode. He took her clit between his lips and sucked on her firmly. She shot off like a rocket. Her hips bucked, and he could see her head thrashing to and fro on the pillow. He growled with satisfaction as she covered his hand with her creamy release.

Seamus couldn't take any more. The need to bury his cock into her tight, wet cunt was paramount. He withdrew his fingers from her ass and pussy, moved up between her lax, splayed thighs, aimed for her cunt, and pushed his hard cock into her dripping pussy. He pumped his cock in and out of her hole a few times, until his erection was coated with her juices, then he withdrew from her body. He nudged Connell off of Leah's breasts, placed his hands on her waist, and turned her until she was lying on her stomach.

"Seamus, what are you doing?" Leah asked, her voice muffled by the pillow until she turned her head to the side and looked at him over her shoulder.

"I want to fuck your ass, darlin'. Do you trust me, Leah?" Seamus asked, waiting with bated breath for her answer.

"Yes. I trust you."

"I was hoping you'd say that, darlin'. I want you to just breathe evenly and deeply. Don't tense up. Try to keep your muscles relaxed. Okay, Leah?"

"Okay."

"Good girl. Connell, hand me the lube."

Seamus took the proffered bottle of lubrication from his brother, flipped the lid, and squirted a generous amount onto the tips of two fingers. He massaged the cold gel into the puckered skin of Leah's ass until she relaxed and he could see the pink ring of muscles. He placed the bottle of lube to her anus and drizzled the viscous liquid into her hole. He cupped his hand, caught the lube in his palm, then coated his hard dick with the gel. He wiped his hand on a small towel his brother gave him, gripped Leah's hips in his hands, and pulled her ass into the air. He covered her body from behind, kissed her on the ear, and slowly but surely began to push his hard cock into her ass.

He groaned as he felt the tight flesh of her ass separate, allowing the head of his cock to pop through into her anus. He held still as her muscles clenched and released around his erection, giving her time to adjust to his invasion.

"Are you okay, darlin'?" Seamus asked against Leah's ear.

"God, yes. Seamus, it burns and pinches, but it feels so good. I want more. Please? I want you to fuck me." Leah sobbed.

"I'll give you more, Leah. But I have to go slow. I don't want to hurt you, baby. How is your arm? Am I hurting you?"

"No. My arm's not hurting at all."

"Good." Seamus growled then pushed his way further into her ass. He felt sweat beading on his brow as he held his control on a tight leash. He was only halfway into Leah's ass, and she was squeezing his cock so hard he was in danger of shooting too soon. He ground his teeth, breathed through his nose, and felt sweat trickle down his nose. He moved his hand around to her pussy and massaged her little clit and then eased his way into her body until his balls were flush with her skin. He held still and wrapped one arm around her waist. The other he placed between her breasts. He lifted her up and pulled her up against his body. He groaned as his cock slid into her ass another inch, and even though he wanted to slide his hard rod in and out of her body, he held still. Leah was now sitting in Seamus's lap with her torso perpendicular to the bed. Her legs were on the outside of his and he moved his wider apart so Connell would have access to her pussy.

Seamus held Leah as his brother moved in closer to their woman. He watched as Connell leaned down and took Leah's mouth with his. When Connell weaned his mouth from Leah's, his brother moved up until Leah's breasts brushed against his brother's chest, and then he felt Connell forging his cock into Leah's cunt. Seamus groaned as her ass got tighter and she clamped down on his erection. Connell was finally buried in her cunt to the hilt, and Seamus held still with his brother, giving their woman time to adjust to the dual invasion.

"Please, please, please," Leah begged.

"Please what, darlin'?" Seamus asked.

"I need you to move," Leah gasped. "Please, now."

Seamus looked over Leah's shoulder and gave Connell a nod. He then pulled his cock from Leah's body and slowly pushed back in. As he advanced, Connell pulled out. He and his brother set up a slow, easy pace. He didn't want to go too fast and hard in case they hurt their woman. He tried to so hard to keep a leash on his libido and control. But with Leah making all those purring, mewling sounds and then beginning to rock her hips between him and his brother, and her internal walls rippling along his hard dick, it was enough to push him over the edge. It seemed his brother was in the same predicament.

Seamus gripped Leah's hips and felt Connell's hands brush his as his brother grasped her rib cage. He withdrew his cock from her ass then slammed back into her. His brother followed, surging into her cunt. Their slow, easy rhythm of slide and glide was shot to hell.

"You are so fucking sexy, Leah," Seamus groaned. "Do you have any idea what it does to me to know me and my brother are loving you together?"

His woman didn't answer him with words. She just moaned and clung onto Connell's biceps as she worked her hips back and forth between them.

Seamus could feel the familiar warning tingle at the base of his spine and knew he wasn't far away from climax. He reached around Leah, slid his hand down her belly between her and Connell's body, being careful not to touch his brother, and gently squeezed her clit between his thumb and finger. She froze in his arms, her neck arching, her head thrown back, and then she screamed.

Leah's pelvic-floor muscles fisted around his cock so hard he felt the cum in his balls boiling as his testicles drew up close to his body, and then he was roaring out his pleasure as he filled her ass with his cum. He heard his brother yell out a moment later and knew their woman had milked the cum from his brother's balls as well.

Seamus felt Leah's twitching body collapse against his, and he wrapped his arms around her, holding her to him tightly. Her head lolled on her neck, and he cupped her chin, tilting her head up so he could see her face. He smiled with masculine pride to see he and his brother had made Leah pass out with pleasure. He eased his cock from her ass, handed her over to Connell, rose on shaky legs, and headed for the bathroom. He cleaned up and then was back to clean Leah up. Once done, he lay beside her in bed, sandwiching her between him and his brother, and knew his life had never been so complete.

Chapter Twelve

Leah was thankful there had been no more incidents for a couple of weeks involving the sicko stalking her. Her arm had healed, and her men were now leaving her alone in the house as they went about their ranch work. They had wanted to stay with her all the time, to take care of her and keep her safe, but Leah had managed to talk them into going back to work. They had been driving her crazy being underfoot all the time, and she had been at her wit's end.

Leah had just finished the housework and was ready to hang out the last load of laundry. She had just stepped out the back door with the basket of clean, wet clothes when she heard a car pull up in the driveway out front. She put the basket down on the timber decking and walked through the house to the front door as the first knock landed. She opened the door and was surprised to find Debbie on the other side.

"You must be Leah. I'm Debbie Newsome. Can I come in?"

Leah debated about slamming the door in the sophisticated woman's face but knew she just didn't have it in her to be that rude. She stepped back, holding the door for the woman to walk through. Leah followed Debbie into the kitchen.

"I'm not here to make trouble if that's what you think," Debbie said as she took a seat at the dining room table.

"Then why are you here?"

"I heard on the grapevine that Connell and Seamus had claimed a woman and was curious. Surely you can understand, I wanted to make sure they hadn't picked some gold digger who was only after their money," Debbie said.

"I don't care about their money. I don't even know if they have any. To be honest with you, Debbie, I love those two men more than my own life. They mean the world to me and I'm not about to let you take them away."

"I can see that you do. Love them, that is. I shouldn't have come back. I knew it was probably too late," Debbie said.

And to Leah's horror Debbie burst into tears. Leah put the coffeepot on with a sigh. It was going to be a long afternoon. Debbie's tears had worn themselves out by the time the coffee was ready. She poured the dark brew into two mugs, gathered cream and sugar, and placed it all on the table.

"Do you want to talk about it?" Leah asked as she sat down.

"Why are you being so nice to me, Leah? No other woman would let an ex into her home," Debbie stated.

"I guess I'm just a glutton for punishment," Leah said with a smile.

"I want to thank you. I came here prepared to rip you to shreds but I just couldn't do it. You're such a beautiful woman, and a nice person," Debbie said.

Leah was taken aback by that statement. Here she was dressed in jeans and a T-shirt, and the woman beside her was dressed to the nines in designer clothes and a perfectly made-up face.

"You know, I don't think I love Connell and Seamus the way you do. I care for them, but I think I just got used to idea of having them close. It was my decision to break up with them because I didn't want the stigma of being labeled a slut by society for having two men. Now that I think about it, I know I wasn't the right woman for them. If I had loved them enough I wouldn't have cared what anyone else thought of our relationship," Debbie said. "You are beautiful on the outside as well as inside."

"Thanks for that. I have always been told I was a fat cow. To hear I'm not from someone like you means a lot," Leah replied. "How long are you going to be in Slick Rock?"

"Well, actually I have just moved from New York and set up residence here. I love the country. I have always dreamed of having my own place and starting a business of my own. My mom recently passed away and since she was my only living relative, I'm now free to pursue my own dreams."

"I'm sorry for your loss," Leah said, covering Debbie's hand with her own. "I know what it's like to lose a loved one."

"Thank you. I can see why they love you, Leah," Debbie replied with a hitch in her voice. "Thanks for the coffee, too. I really should get going."

Leah followed Debbie out to the front door and watched as the woman hesitated on the doorstep.

"I'd really like for us to be friends if that is at all possible, Leah. I don't know anyone else besides you, Seamus, and Connell."

"I think I can do that. What sort of business are you planning on?" Leah asked.

Leah watched as Debbie's cheeks turned red. She had never thought to see that reaction from such a sophisticated woman.

"I was thinking of opening a ladies' lingerie and toy store," Debbie replied.

"Really? That's the last thing I would have thought of but I can see that would suit you to a T," Leah replied with a laugh. "You go, girl. I'd love to help you set up your store. Give me a call when you're ready to start."

"Thank you, Leah. I really like you," Debbie said then walked down the steps toward her car. She turned to Leah and waved then got in her car and drove away.

Who'd have thought that she would wind up friends with her men's ex? Usually it wasn't heard of, but Leah decided she liked the sophisticated, vulnerable woman. She could see that Debbie's polish was a front and wondered what had made her into the woman she was. Maybe one day Debbie would confide in her. Leah closed the door and went to hang out the laundry.

* * * *

Leah had everything prepared for dinner and put the large tray of lasagna in the oven on low. She reached for the bag of ground coffee and saw there wasn't enough left for another pot. She searched through the pantry but couldn't find another bag. She was going to have to borrow one of her men's trucks and head into town. She set the timer on the oven to turn off automatically so the lasagna wouldn't burn, grabbed her purse and keys, and stepped outside. She knew she'd have plenty of time to get to town and back before her men got home.

Leah drove to town, bought the coffee, and had just unlocked the truck, when a man's voice came from behind her. She turned to see who was talking to her.

"Excuse me, ma'am, I was wondering if you'd be kind enough to give me some of your time."

"I beg your pardon?" Leah replied as she looked the stranger up and down. He was dressed in suave designer slacks, black Italian leather moccasin-type shoes, and he had on a shirt which could have come off the cover of a *GQ* magazine. He gave her the creeps. She looked around, but there were no cars or people on the street. He was so close to her now that if she so much as breathed she would be touching him. Leah was about to step around the man, but a firm object poking into her stomach made her freeze. She looked down to see the barrel of a gun pressed against her belly.

"Who are you? What do you want?" Leah asked, hearing the quaver in her own voice.

"You and I are going for a little drive, Leah. Get in the truck and don't try and scream or I'll shoot you right here, right now."

Leah was shaking so much she could barely get her body to obey her brain's command. She turned toward the truck, opened the door, and got in. The stranger got in beside her and pushed her over to the passenger side of the vehicle.

"Give me the keys," the stranger demanded. "Now, you slut."

Leah handed the keys over and reached for the door handle. She had to get out of here. She didn't know what she'd done to piss the man off, but she could see the fury in his eyes. She'd never even met him.

"Don't even think about it. I'll pull the trigger and put a bullet between your eyes before you even have the door open." The stranger growled at her.

The stranger turned the key, and then he backed out of the parking lot. Leah was so scared she couldn't think properly. She knew she had to do something to get away from him, but had no idea what. She took some deep, calming breaths and clenched her hands around her purse. *That's it.* She needed to find her cell phone and call Seamus or Connell. They had programmed their cell numbers into her phone on speed dial. All she needed to do was push a button and pray to God the man wouldn't hear her phone beeping. Maybe if she could get him talking she could cover up what she was doing?

"Why are you doing this? I don't even know you. So I can't have done anything to piss you off."

"It's not you I'm pissed at. It's those fucking O'Hara assholes."

"What did they do?" Leah asked and slowly slid her hand into her purse.

"They took my woman away from me and then dumped her. If they hadn't come on the scene Debbie and I would be married by now."

"Did you ever stop to think that they wouldn't have been able to take Debbie away from you if she had really loved you?" Leah asked without thinking.

The hand the stranger held the gun in rose and smashed into her cheek.

"Shut the fuck up. Just shut up or I'll kill you now," the stranger screamed.

Leah's cheek throbbed where he had just belted her one. She wanted to reach over and claw at his face and eyes, but knew she would be dead before she could even try.

"You know they will come for me, don't you? They're going to find you and hunt you down. You don't stand a chance," Leah said loudly as she felt her cell phone, ran her fingers over the number pad, and pushed the button. She hoped she had pushed the right one, but without being able to look she couldn't be sure.

"That's what you think. I've been planning this for years. You coming on the scene only made it easier. I want them to come for me. That's what I planned all along. You and me are going to have a little party. They are going to find your dead body and be so consumed with guilt they'll just walk right on into my trap."

Shit. Leah wondered what he had planned. The last thing she wanted was for her men to walk into a trap because of her. She wondered if her cell phone had connected and was about to disconnect the line, but then she remembered her men talking about being in the service. They were both trained lethal weapons. Her men were ex-Marines, and she knew they would take into account all possible scenarios. She took her finger off her phone and prayed to God they could hear her.

"You can't make someone love you," Leah said louder than usual. "If Debbie left you then it wasn't right."

"I told you to keep your fucking mouth shut, slut. I'll just have to shut it for you," the stranger snarled.

Leah saw the fist coming, but she wasn't fast enough. He slammed his knuckles into her cheek, temple, and the side of her eye socket. Pain exploded through her head, and she knew she was going to pass out. She fought against the darkness. She breathed deeply and finally the black spots before her eyes left, but she closed her eyes and slumped against the door. She was playing possum until she got her chance to escape.

Chapter Thirteen

Connell removed his cell phone from his belt and looked at the name displayed on the screen. He smiled and answered then placed the phone to his ear. At first he couldn't hear anything and wondered if Leah had accidentally activated her phone. The smile left his face when he heard Leah yelling and then a man's voice yelling back. *Fuck.* Leah was in trouble. Connell covered the mouthpiece on his phone and whistled for Seamus. He only ever whistled when there was danger, and he knew his brother would be at his side in moments.

"Leah's in trouble," Connell stated. "Call Luke and Damon to meet us back at the house. She's such a smart little thing. She called me on her cell. I need to keep the phone glued to my ear, but we need to get back to the house."

Connell urged his mount into a gallop. His brother was behind him the whole way. By the time he reached the yard, Luke and Damon, as well as Damon's two brothers, Sam and Tyson, were pulling up into the yard. They were all ex-Marines, except for Sheriff Luke Sun-Walker, but he was just as tough as the rest of them.

"I have Leah on my cell. She was yelling and I heard a man yelling back, but I couldn't work out what they were saying," Connell said as he swung down from his horse and handed his mount over to a ranch hand.

"Connell, your truck's gone," Seamus said, pointing in the direction of the carport.

"Shit. Wait, I have a GPS tracker in the truck. Luke, can you get onto that and find out where they're headed? I can't hear anything at the moment. It's gone quiet. Fuck it. Who could have taken her? Let's go inside and see what we can find out," Connell said and led the way into the house. He placed his cell on speaker but made sure to mute the microphone. He listened intently but could only hear a faint droning sound.

"It sounds like road noise, but muffled," Damon said.

"She must have her cell in her purse. Goddamn it," Connell roared and slammed his fist on the table. "I knew we shouldn't have left her alone. We have no idea who even has her."

"Keep it together, man," Damon said, placing a hand on Connell's shoulder. "You're trained to deal with this shit. Calm down and think."

"I put an APB out on your truck and it was spotted heading west out of town. I've just called Clay and Johnny Morten from the Double M ranch, as well as Billy and Tom on the Double E, to be on the lookout since their ranches are west. Billy told me he saw your truck driving past in the distance. So let's head on out," Luke commanded.

Connell and Seamus jumped into Luke's four-by-four. Connell had never felt so scared in his life. The fact that someone had taken his woman had a knot bigger than a fist sitting in his gut. He wanted to rage and yell and lose control of his emotions, but his friend Damon was right. He was trained to deal with this sort of trouble, and emotion had no place in this situation. He breathed deeply and evenly, pushed his emotions to the back of his mind, and became the cold, calculating killing machine he had been trained to be. He looked at Seamus and saw his brother going through the same struggle he was. Then his brother's eyes got real cold, and he knew Seamus was back in control. He was determined to have Leah back in his arms, and if he had to die trying to free her, then so be it.

* * * *

Leah kept her head turned away from the man in the driver's seat of the truck. She just hoped he wouldn't notice she had one eye open and was watching where he was taking her. She had nearly given away her advantage when they had driven past a cowboy tending a fence in the distance, but had stopped herself from moving at the last minute. The cowboy had been too far away, and there was nothing he could have done to help her. Leah prayed to God her men had realized she was missing by now and had called the sheriff. She was scared of the man, could see he wasn't right in the mind, but she wasn't about to let fear consume her. She thought of Seamus and Connell, which seemed to fill her with hope and strength. She pushed the fear and panic away and began to get angry.

How dare this bastard use her as a pawn in his sick game! She hadn't done anything wrong, and neither had Debbie. This sick fuck was obviously obsessed with the woman who had spurned him, and he couldn't deal with reality. She'd had enough. Leah moaned and moved her head to the seat headrest, then let her muscles go lax again, making sure to breathe evenly and deeply, hoping the bastard would think she was still out cold. After a few minutes she opened her eyes to slits, using her lashes to shield the fact her eyes weren't closed anymore. She saw the gun resting on the seat between them. He had both hands on the steering wheel as he drove around a tight bend. Leah didn't stop to think. She just reacted. She picked up the gun and had the barrel against the man's temple before he could react.

"Stop the car now," Leah demanded in a cold voice.

He surprised her by giving her a smile, and then his words washed over her.

"Go ahead and shoot. You'll likely end up dead when the car crashes."

Leah didn't hesitate. She pulled the trigger. Nothing happened. The car slowed and stopped in the middle of the road. He whipped the gun out of her hand and tilted the gun to the side. His cold smile had chills running up and down her spine.

"You forgot about the safety. This little button here takes it off," he said, and Leah watched as he depressed the button. "Get out of the car and don't try anything or I'll kill you here."

Leah was shaking so much it took her three tries to get the door handle to open. She slid from the truck, about to take off, but a large hand clamped around her wrist. She hadn't even heard him get out behind her. He shoved her off the road toward the open field before her and the hill in the distance. He pushed and shoved, knocking her down at every opportunity. At one stage Leah had been so angry she'd turned around to hit the bastard, but she had ended up staring down the barrel of his gun. The sight of that hollowed-out steel had her knees going weak and her body shaking with fear. He slapped her across the face again, and Leah ended up on her back in the grass. Her face and head were throbbing so much she was in danger of becoming sick. She knew if she was ill she was going to try and aim for him.

It seemed to take forever before they reached the slight hill with large rocks strewn about. His voice stopped her in her tracks.

"Get up on that flat rock and lie down."

Leah didn't have much choice since he was holding a gun on her, but she wasn't going down without a fight. She kept her eyes on the ground and stumbled when she saw a small, sharp piece of rock. She picked it up and held it in her hand as he hauled her to her feet by her hair. She didn't give him the satisfaction of crying out when he hurt her. He pushed her to the large, flat rock, and as she turned around, she saw the rope and metal pegs in his other hand. She hadn't seen them before and wondered how she had missed them. "Get on that rock, you slut."

Leah crawled onto the rock, still clutching the sharp shard of stone in her hand. He pushed her onto her back, placed the gun in the waistband of his pants, and moved around to her head. Leah gripped the piece of sharp stone so tightly she felt it cut into her hand. She ignored the pain and swung with all her might. She put everything she had into the swing and yelled as her fist connected with the bastard's nose. Blood spurted from his nostrils, and the sound of his pained yell gave her a cold satisfaction as she scrambled from the rock. She ran and didn't look back. She ducked into the line of trees ten yards from the rocks and kept right on running. She felt a fierce, stinging pain in the back of her upper thigh but ignored it. Adrenaline was pumping through her body, and she used it to get as far away from him as she could.

Leah cried out as she tripped over a tree root and tumbled to the ground. She pushed up to her feet, only to fall back down again. Her right leg was hurting like a bitch, the burning pain so intense she felt sick to her stomach. She heaved and sobbed as pain tore through her thigh. She tried to see what was wrong, but she couldn't turn her head around far enough. She heard the crackling of feet amongst the dead leaves and grass on the ground and knew she was in danger again. He'd found her.

She cried out when he grabbed a handful of her hair and began to drag her back to the clearing where the large, flat rock was. He had her bound and gagged on the rock before she could blink.

She was so cold and tired. She wanted to close her eyes and sleep. She knew she had to stay awake, but couldn't remember why. She opened her eyes and blinked a few times as bright sunlight hurt her pupils. Leah couldn't remember where she was, but knew she was in danger. She curled her hands into fists and felt something sharp cut into the soft skin of her palm. Memory slammed into her mind. She had been kidnapped and she was laid out on a large, flat rock like a lamb on an altar. She looked around but couldn't see anyone. She knew he was still there, somewhere. Watching and waiting for her men to show up. She could see he had the advantage. Her men would be coming from the road, and he was hidden amongst the trees just waiting to take them out. She couldn't let that happen. Not now. She'd only just found the loves of her life, and there was no way in hell he was going to hurt them.

Leah used her fingers to get the bit of sharp stone to her fingertips and began to work on the rope around her wrist. She was getting out of here and saving her men if it was the last thing she did.

Chapter Fourteen

Connell was the first out of Luke's truck when he found his abandoned in the middle of the road. He checked his truck out and was relieved to find no signs of struggle or any blood in the vehicle. He searched around and found what he was looking for, two sets of footprints leading to the open field. He was about to take off across the open plain, but Seamus's hand on his shoulder stopped him.

"Tom Eagle just called Luke. It's a trap, Connell. Billy was the one who saw your truck pass by earlier, and when he got the call from the sheriff he followed the vehicle through the paddocks on horseback, keeping amongst the trees for camouflage. Luke got a call from Tom, just as you got out of the truck. Billy called his brother and told him what's going on. He heard a gunshot and then he saw that fucker dragging Leah onto a large rock. He wanted to go in and take him down, but Billy is unarmed and he didn't want to put Leah in jeopardy. That sick fuck is using Leah as bait to draw us out.

"Whoever took Leah has her tied down on a rock on that hill. They are looking for the bastard, but he's hiding in the trees waiting for us. No doubt he's got a high-powered rifle ready and waiting for us to show up," Seamus explained.

"You think I don't know that. I can't leave her out there alone, Seamus. She has to be so scared. God, I just want to hold her in my arms," Connell said and knew he'd let the anguish he felt show in his voice.

"Hey, I do, too, man. But we have to keep our heads clear if we're going to get her out of this," Seamus replied.

"I know that. I just…My gut won't let up, Seamus. She's hurt and I need to see her. To be with her and hold her."

"I know, Connell. Now, get it together again or you're going to blow this," Seamus said.

Connell took slow, deep, even breaths, getting his fear and anxiety under control once more. He turned and faced his brother and knew he was back to being that cold, calculating killing machine he had been trained to be when Seamus slapped him on the shoulder. He and Seamus moved over to the others.

"Whoever it is that took Leah is hiding in the trees. Billy from the Double E Ranch followed him, but lost him when he slid amongst the bushes. He and his brother, Tom Eagle, as well as Clay and Johnny Morten, from the Double M Ranch, are searching for the bastard. Tom called Clay and explained the situation and they volunteered to help.

"We should go into the line of trees over there and work our way up to the rise. I don't want that bastard seeing us by walking out in the open. Hopefully we'll spot him as we move. We need to get to Leah as quickly as possible, but we don't want any casualties. Let's move out and stay out of sight," Luke commanded.

Connell followed Luke and Damon, Seamus at his side, and Tyson and Sam brought up the rear. They were all packing as much firepower and as many knives as they could carry in their clothes and boots. They were all now in warrior mode, and nothing was going to stop them from catching their prey. They moved silently and stealthily through the trees, being careful of where they placed their feet. The last thing they wanted to do was alert the bastard they were after him, if he wasn't already aware. There were no birds singing amongst the trees. The only sound was the swish of leaves in the breeze as they moved. They were like ghosts in the wind.

* * * *

Leah was so cold she was shaking. She knew there was something terribly wrong with her leg, but she didn't have time to stop and worry about that now. She needed to free herself so her men wouldn't be used as sitting ducks when they came for her. Her fingers were so sliced up and covered with blood she'd nearly lost her small shard of stone several times. Her heart dropped down into her stomach each time the bit of rock nearly slipped out of her fingers. She felt as if she'd been working at cutting the rope around her wrist for hours. She had no concept of time at all, but she was determined to get free and not be a lure to trap her men.

Leah felt the rope around her wrist slip again and tugged with every bit of strength she had left. She nearly cried out with joy when the rope gave way. She moved her now-free hand to the rope around her other wrist and worked to undo the knot. She felt it slide off her red, abraded skin, and instead of sitting up, leaving herself as an easy target, she contorted her body around so she could reach the rope at her ankles.

Her head felt woozy when she moved, and she was so tired she wanted to lie down and sleep, but she didn't have that luxury. She got back to work. The first knot around her ankle came undone easily. The second knot was so tight, and she couldn't get her fingers to cooperate to pull it off. She lifted her head up and looked around her. She decided she could slide off the rock to the front where she would be out of sight of the tree line and work on the rope when she was hidden.

She used her arms and hands as well as the leg that wasn't hurting to push and pull her body to the front edge of the rock. She gave one last push, using the last of her strength, and fell off the rock to the ground. She bit her lip as agony, white-hot excruciating pain, radiated down her thigh and the entire length of her leg. The pain was so bad she thought she was going to throw up or pass out. She panted through the pain and tried to keep herself conscious. She needed to get the last rope off. That task became her focus. She obsessed over it.

She was so out of it now, finding it hard to concentrate, and forgot she was out of sight of the tree line at her back, hidden completely from view. She twisted her body until she was bent in half and pulled at the rope knot with her cold, numb fingers. She passed out just as the knot slid free.

* * * *

Connell could feel the bastard close by. He stood completely still, his breathing shallow so it couldn't be heard. The others were nearby, and they had frozen in their tracks as well. His eyes searched the trees from the ground up to the top branches, but he couldn't see him. He could feel that time was running out, a gut instinct he didn't push aside. There was only one option. He was going to have to draw the bastard out. He moved away from his brother and the other men, not making a sound. He was careful of where he placed his feet and made sure his clothes didn't brush anything. He could see Seamus looking at him with anger, but knew his brother was aware of his plan. Once he was far enough away from the others, he stepped on a twig. The sound was like gunshot fire, echoing through the trees, being carried on the wind. He held still for a bare moment then dove to his left behind a large tree limb which had fallen to the ground.

He'd been wrong. Gunshot fire was so much louder than the twig cracking. The sound of a man screaming in agony followed the shot, and then a loud thud followed that. The bastard had just fallen from his perch to the ground.

Connell didn't worry about the fallen man. His one and only intent was to get to his woman. Now that the danger was over, stealth went to the wayside. He ran as though the hounds of hell were chasing him and burst from the tree line. The sight of so much blood on the flat rock nearly had his knees buckling out from beneath him. He ran around the large outcropping and roared with anguish.

Leah lay crumpled on the ground. Her body twisted unnaturally, and she was covered with blood. He pulled her into his arms and began to rock her. He was careless of the tears streaming down his face.

"Connell, we have to see to Leah. Let me take a look at her so we can fix her up." Seamus growled.

His brother's anguished voice cut through Connell like a knife. He had to get it together again for his woman. He lowered Leah so her head was resting in his lap, but he got to work helping his brother. She still had a pulse. It was faint and fast, but she was still alive. He helped Seamus to get Leah onto her side as gently as possible and they began to work.

Seamus found the site of her wound and cut away her jeans with a knife as he watched. She had been shot. The bullet had gone into the back of her thigh and was still embedded in her flesh. Connell tore off his shirt, bunched it up, leaned down, and pressed it against her injury. He saw Seamus remove his own shirt and tie it as tight as he could around Leah's thigh. Damon's voice had him and his brother looking up.

"The paramedics are on the way. We need to get her down to the roadside."

Connell shifted to his knees and carefully lifted Leah into his arms. He was on the move before anyone could stop him. The sound of a helicopter overhead had his stomach knotting again, but he knew Leah would be in the best of hands. It was going to take over an hour to get to the large hospital a few towns over, and he didn't think he was up for the drive. No, he was getting on that chopper with his woman, come hell or high water.

The copter landed, and instead of waiting for the paramedics, Connell ran the last of the distance, carefully placing Leah on the stretcher. He moved to the side of the chopper and watched as the paramedics got to work. He sighed with relief as they took off. He had expected the paramedics to tell him there wasn't enough room for him. They hooked Leah up to a drip and began to work on her battered, injured body. One of the men worked on her gunshot wound as the other placed the heart-monitor tags to her chest. Connell couldn't hear the sounds of the heart monitor, but he watched as the lines jumped with her pulse across the screen. Once the paramedics had her stabilized, there wasn't much else they could do. The rest was up to the doctors, Leah, and God Himself.

Chapter Fifteen

Connell had paced the corridor outside the surgery theater for what seemed like hours. He rubbed a hand down his face again and then turned toward the corridor when he heard heavy footsteps. His brother and Luke, Damon, Tyson, and Sam, as well as Billy, Tom, Clay, and Johnny, were all moving down the hallway, in his direction. He saw the nurses at the station stop whatever they were doing to openly ogle his brother and friends.

"Is there any news?" Seamus asked.

"No. I've about had enough. I've been as patient as I can. I was about to burst through those doors to find out what was going on just as you arrived," Connell replied.

"Fuck it. She was in a bad way, Connell. Surely there is someone who can tell us what is going on." Seamus growled, and Connell watched his brother pace with frustration.

Just as Seamus turned to head back toward him, Connell heard the doors to the operating theatre open. He turned to face the doctor.

"Are you with Ms. Harmer?"

"Yes, she's our fiancée," Connell replied and was glad when the doctor didn't balk or show any expression to his statement.

"I'm Dr. Wayne Plante," he said and offered his hand in greeting.

"How is she, doctor?"

"It was touch and go for a while. Leah had lost a lot of blood. The bullet had nicked a major artery and we nearly lost her. She's a fighter though, which is good. We got the bullet out and have her patched up. The bullet didn't hit her femur, which is a plus. We've got her hitched up to an intravenous drip. We're pumping her full of antibiotics to stave off infection, as well as saline. We had to give her blood, and she seems to be responding well. I'm not going to lie to you, but it's up to Leah now. Her survival is in her hands and the hand of God. The next twenty-four hours are the most critical, and if she makes it through those, then she is well on the way to recovery."

Connell's legs felt so weak at the doctor's information he was in danger of having to sit down, but he knew he had to be strong for Leah.

"Can we see her?" Connell asked, his voice so low and raspy even he didn't recognize it.

"Yes. A nurse will be out in a few minutes. We're just getting Leah into the intensive care unit. If you have any questions, don't hesitate to call me," Dr. Plante said, handing over his business card.

"Thanks, doctor," Connell replied and watched as he left.

"Fuck it, Connell. We only just found her. We can't lose her now," Seamus whispered.

"I know, brother. I know," Connell replied.

A nurse appeared a few minutes later and led Connell and Seamus to where Leah was resting. She looked so small and helpless. Connell felt tears forming in his eyes again. He didn't care that he was crying over the sight of his woman lying on that hospital bed, so small and pale. She was hooked up to more machines than he could count, and she had needles taped to the back of both hands. He wanted to yell and rage, but he knew that wouldn't help his woman. He grabbed a chair from against the wall and pulled it close to the bed. He sat down and slid his hand beneath one of hers. The feel of her cool flesh on his had his heart clenching with fear. He was careful not to touch the needle in her hand, but he rubbed his thumb back and forth over the exposed skin. She was so precious to him. He didn't know what he would do if she left them. He placed his head on the bed and bawled his eyes out.

Connell must have fallen asleep, because a light hand to his shoulder had him jerking upright. A young nurse stood over him and smiled kindly at him.

"Why don't you go and get some sleep? I'll call you if there is any change."

"No. Thanks anyway but I'm not going anywhere," Connell replied.

He sat back in his chair and looked across the bed to see his brother was asleep. His head was resting on the bed, and he was holding Leah's hand. He glanced at his watch and was surprised to see it was three in the morning. He hadn't been asleep long. After he'd cried out his anguish, he sat staring at Leah, willing her to fight, and he'd prayed. He'd never really believed in God, not with all the fighting he'd been in and the murder and destruction he'd seen. But he vowed if Leah pulled through he would become as devout as the Pope.

He must have fallen asleep again. Seamus woke him up and handed him a cup of coffee. The sun was streaming through the windows as if nothing bad had touched his life or the world. He sat with Leah's hand in his as he sipped his coffee. He had never felt so useless in his life. There was nothing he or his brother could do to help their woman now. It was all up to her.

Visitors dropped in over the next few hours, each of them wanting to know how Leah was. Luke and Damon had come by to let them know the bastard, Shayne Green, who had abducted and wounded her was out to hurt him and his brother. It seemed he had been in a relationship with their ex, Debbie, and, since he had been obsessed with the woman, had vowed to get back at them for taking her away from him. Luke had told him the man was off his rocker and had been committed into a mental institution after having the gunshot wound to his arm seen to. He felt guilty about that, and even though he knew it wasn't his or Seamus's fault, the guilt had him feeling sick to his stomach. The hours wore on, and Connell was getting scared Leah wasn't going to wake up.

The nursing staff didn't seem to be worried that she slept so long, and the doctor had been in a few times to check on her. When Connell had questioned the doctor, he had told him Leah was in a healing sleep and probably wouldn't awaken for another twenty-four hours. That didn't ease Connell's mind at all. He ran his hand down his face, his stubble rasping against his hand. He knew he probably looked like hell and was in dire need of a shower but he didn't care. Luke had bought him and Seamus each a T-shirt to put on, and he was glad he didn't have to go around half dressed. The sound of a low moan had his head spinning on his shoulders. He looked up to Leah, and then the hand he was holding pulled at the oxygen mask on her face. He felt joy and hope filling his heart. The sight of his woman moving was the best thing he'd seen in his life. He rose to his feet and moved up to the head of the bed. He bent down and kissed her on the forehead, and then he whispered in her ear.

"I love you so much, baby. You're going to be fine. Seamus is here with me. We've been so worried about you. You're in the hospital, Leah. Just rest and get better," Connell said and kissed her again.

Leah's fingers tugged at the mask, obviously trying to remove it. Connell lifted it from her face and let it fall around her neck.

"Water," Leah whispered.

Connell felt tears leaking out of his eyes. That was the best word he'd heard in a long time. He knew then that Leah was going to be all right. He leaned down and spoke quietly in her ear again.

"I'll get you some water, baby. I just have to go ask one of the nurses. I'll be back in a minute. Okay? Seamus will keep you company while I'm gone."

Connell was off like a shot. He hurried to the nurse's station and knew he probably looked like a fool with stubble coating his face and his clothes rumpled, and he probably smelled even worse, but he didn't give a shit. His Leah was awake.

After assuring the nurses would bring Leah ice chips and then water, Connell hurried back to his woman. Connell hesitated in the door as he watched Seamus weeping all over Leah. He knew if he hadn't already, he would be bawling alongside his brother. Leah had her fingers on Seamus's scalp, running them through his brother's short blond hair. It touched his heart to see their woman comforting his brother when she was still so weak. Her face was still pale, she was hooked up to machines and drips, but she was comforting Seamus. God, what a woman!

Connell moved up to Leah's side and took her hand in his. She squeezed his hand, and he looked down to see her eyes open to slits and a small smile on her face. She had never looked so beautiful.

The nurse came bustling in, a jug of water in one hand and a cup of ice chips in the other. She smiled at him, and his brother placed the items on the table and left them alone.

Connell picked up the cup of ice chips with the spoon and held the utensil to Leah's dry, cracked lips. She moaned as she opened her mouth, her tongue flicking out to capture the moisture. She licked over her dry lips and came back for more ice chips. Connell knew when she shook her head slightly she'd had enough. He watched as her eyes drifted closed again and she slid back into the healing sleep.

Leah woke on and off throughout the day, and every time she woke he or Seamus was ready with the ice. She graduated to water by the time the sun set, and Connell felt weariness tugging at him.

"You look exhausted. How long have you been here?" Leah rasped out.

"A couple of days, baby," Connell answered.

"Why don't you go and get some sleep? I'm going to be fine," Leah stated.

Connell hesitated. He knew they should catch up on a bit of sleep so he and Seamus could take care of Leah when she was ready to go home, but he didn't want to leave her.

"Connell, I'm fine. I promise. I'm not going anywhere. Go and get some sleep and clean up. You'll feel a lot better," Leah said.

"Are you telling me I smell, baby?" Connell asked with a smile.

"Well, I don't think it's me," Leah replied. "Go on. I'm just going to go back to sleep. By the time you've had a sleep and a shower, maybe I'll be ready to stay awake longer."

"Okay. We'll go, but get the nurses to call us if you need us or want anything. Okay?" Connell asked.

"I promise," Leah replied, her eyes closing once more.

"I love you, baby," Connell stated.

"Love you, too," Leah slurred.

"I love you, darlin'," Seamus said.

"Love you," Leah replied, and then Connell heard her breathing deepen as she drifted off.

Chapter Sixteen

She heard heavy footsteps outside and looked up as they walked in the door to her room. She had been unhooked from all the tubes and wires the previous night and was about to go have a shower.

Leah was kept in the hospital for another four days. Her men had booked a room at a motel and left her each night to sleep. She was glad she had encouraged them to seek rest that first night she had awoken to find them at her side. They had looked worse than she felt, and she had been worried about them. The day of her release had taken too long to come around, and she was itching to get out of the place. The stitches in the back of her thigh had just been removed, and she was anxious to see her men.

Seamus reached her first and kissed her on the head as he gave her a hug.

"Hey, darlin'. How are you feeling?"

"I'm fine," Leah said and hugged Seamus back.

He released her, and Connell took his place.

"Hi, baby. I love you," Connell said, giving her a hug and kissing her head.

"I love you, too."

"Well, Leah. It's good to see you looking so perky. By the time you've showered and dressed, the paperwork for your release should be done and you can get out of here," Dr. Plante stated from just inside the door. "You two are looking much better as well."

"Thanks for all your help, doctor," Connell said and offered his hand.

Leah watched as her men thanked the doctor who had saved her life, and then the doctor left them alone.

"Let's get you cleaned up, baby, and get on home," Connell said.

"I don't think you're supposed to be helping me in the shower," Leah said and felt her cheeks heat with a blush.

"I'm not leaving you alone in there by yourself, baby. You could slip and hurt yourself. Come on, I'll help you. Seamus and I bought you some new clothes to go home in," Connell said and helped her to stand.

When Leah wavered on her feet, Connell scooped her up into his arms and carried her through to the bathroom. He placed her on the shower chair and stepped over to the faucets and handheld showerhead. He turned the head so when he turned the taps on, the water sprayed against the tile wall. He came back to her and helped her remove her hospital gown. He wouldn't let her do a thing. He washed her from top to bottom and all the way in between. He even washed her hair. Leah sat and enjoyed the way his fingers gently massaged her scalp and couldn't help but moan at the sensation.

"There'll be none of that, baby. Not until you get the all clear from Doc back in Slick Rock," Connell said and rinsed the suds from her hair.

Once done, he wrapped her in a large towel and began to dry her hair with another. He scooped her up and carried her out to the room. She was thankful Seamus had closed the door, because she could feel her ass hanging out from the towel. Connell carried her over to the bed and gently sat her on the side. He and Seamus closed the curtains around the bed and began to help her dress.

"I can do all this myself, you know," Leah said.

"We know you can, darlin'. We just need to feel useful. And the doctor said you weren't to do too much, 'cos you were going to feel tired for a while to come," Seamus answered.

"I know, but that doesn't mean you have to carry me or do everything for me. How am I going to get my strength back if you won't let me do anything?"

"We will eventually, baby. We just…I can still see you lying on that bed so pale, Leah. You nearly died for fuck's sake. We need to do this for you. Okay? Just have a little patience for a couple of days," Connell said as he buttoned her shirt.

"Okay. I'll try, but you can't keep mollycoddling me forever. You'll end up pissing me off," Leah replied.

"I'd rather have you pissed at me than having you relapse because you did too much." Connell growled.

Leah sighed. She knew they were going to drive her crazy, and she was going to let them. For a couple of days, anyway.

"Did you bring a brush or a comb?" Leah asked as she tried to finger comb her hair.

She watched Seamus reach into the large plastic bag he'd taken the clothes from and produced a hairbrush. She reached for it, only to have it snatched away.

"That's my job, darlin'. Just sit back and enjoy," Seamus said and crawled onto the bed behind her. He brushed her hair thoroughly and was so gentle she hardly felt the bristles sliding over her scalp. When he was done, Seamus produced a toothbrush and toothpaste. She snatched them from his hand and slid off the bed. She'd been using small disposable brushes and the worst-tasting toothpaste she'd ever encountered. She was going to scrub her mouth until her teeth shone and her tongue stung. She was in the bathroom before either of her men could stop her.

"I'm going to tan your ass for that move, baby. You should have let me carry you into the bathroom. I saw you wobbling on your feet. You have to take it slowly, Leah. Don't be in too much of a rush to be independent before you feel up to it. When Doc gives you the all clear I'm going to turn those lush, fleshy globes pink," Connell said as he moved up behind her.

"In your dreams, pal," Leah said but knew Connell hadn't understood a word she'd said since she had a mouthful of toothbrush and toothpaste. She gave him the raised eyebrow though, because he gave a sexy wink and smile.

Leah was ready to head out when one of the nurses entered the room.

"Your paperwork is all done. You're free to leave."

"Thank God. Oh, sorry. Thanks so much for taking such good care of me," Leah said with a wry smile.

The nurse laughed at her and replied, "No problem, Leah. I don't want to see you back here again."

"No offense, but I don't want to see me back here either," Leah answered.

The nurse leaned down and whispered in her ear. "Your men are drop-dead gorgeous." Leah felt her cheeks heat and her heart fill with love and pride for them. She agreed with the nurse. She was one lucky lady.

Leah said good-bye to the nurse and sat in the wheelchair just outside the door with a grimace. She couldn't understand hospital policy of wheeling all patients off the premises, but she knew if she tried to walk, one of her men would pick her up and carry her. As much as she loved being in their arms, she didn't want to make a spectacle of herself, so she sat quietly and let them wheel her out. She breathed in the fresh air and closed her eyes as the cool autumn breeze enveloped her. She could smell sage and ozone and knew it was going to rain soon. She was so glad to be free of the antiseptic smell of the hospital.

"Wait here, darlin'. I'll go get the truck," Seamus said, leaned down, and kissed her on the lips then took off.

"Where did he think I was going to go?" Leah asked.

"Nowhere, baby. He's just taking care of you. Here he is. Let's get you settled. Do you want to ride in the front or the back, baby?" Connell asked.

"In the front with you and Seamus," Leah answered. "I've missed you both so much."

"The front it is," Connell replied and scooped her up into his arms. The feel of his muscles rippling had her pussy weeping onto her new panties.

Connell eased her into the truck beside Seamus and buckled her in. He got in beside her, wrapped his arm around her shoulder, and pulled her against his side.

"You all set, darlin'?" Seamus asked.

"Yeah, let's go home," Leah replied and snuggled up to Connell.

She was finally going home, where she belonged.

Chapter Seventeen

"Leah, are you ready?" Connell's voice called down the hallway.

They were driving Leah insane. Connell and Seamus hadn't left her side since they had brought her home from the hospital. It had been five long days, but it felt more like ten. They wouldn't let her lift a finger. She had tried to sneak, lie, and cheat her way into being able to do something other than rest, but they always caught her. They had hired another two ranch hands to take over their work and tried to keep her entertained, but she was sick and tired of being treated like a child. They wouldn't even let her make a cup of coffee without giving her the third degree. She was wound so tight she felt like she was going to explode. Something had to give, and she didn't want it to be her. She had been so patient with them, but enough was enough. She was about ready to leave for her appointment with Doc and knew, once she had the all clear, she was taking a stand.

"Yes, I'm coming," Leah replied. She took one last look in the mirror on her dresser, grabbed her purse, and headed to the kitchen-dining room where her men were waiting for her.

Connell and Seamus turned toward her as she entered the room. They were so fucking hot just the sight of them had her creaming her panties. She took a deep breath and headed for the back door.

"Come on, let's get this done," Leah said. She followed them out and was in the truck before she'd had a chance to reach the last step. Connell had done it again. He'd literally picked her up and put her in the truck. He got in beside her as Seamus got into the driver's seat. Leah ground her teeth together in frustration, but kept her mouth closed. The last thing she wanted to do was start an argument in the close confines of the truck.

"Are you okay, darlin'?" Seamus asked as he moved the gear stick and began to drive.

"I'm fine," Leah replied testily.

"What's with the attitude, baby?" Connell asked from her other side.

"I don't have any attitude," Leah replied coolly.

"Now, that's just a lie. You've been snapping and snarly at us for the last couple of days," Connell replied.

"Just leave it, Connell. Now is not the time or the place," Leah snapped.

"You're just begging for a spanking, baby," Connell said and ran a finger down her cheek.

"Connell, leave off, all right? I'm not in the mood to deal with you right now."

Connell gave her that look, the one where he raised his eyebrow, which told her she was pushing him to his limit. Leah didn't care. She was way beyond her own limit. She was so mad at them right now she wanted to scream and rage, but she knew she'd just be wasting her breath. Instead she stared out the front windscreen of the truck, counting in her head as she tried to control her anger. She took another few deep breaths and let them out slowly. She felt her tight muscles loosen slightly, giving her a little reprieve from the restless energy permeating her body.

By the time Seamus pulled the truck into the parking lot of Doc's office, she was more in control of her simmering temper. Connell helped her out of the truck, and she turned away from him without thanking him. She just wanted to get the all clear from Doc and move on with her life.

Leah was thankful Doc's office was empty, and she was able to go straight into his rooms. She sat patiently waiting for the elderly man to give her the once-over, finally pronouncing her fit and healthy.

Then the questions started. Leah was so embarrassed by the intimate questions Connell and Seamus asked Doc, and she felt her cheeks flame. The heat in her cheeks was so hot she wondered if she was going to blow a gasket. By the time they left Doc's office and headed back home, Leah was a seething mass of rage. She sat between Seamus and Connell, breathing heavily as she stared out the front window. No matter what she did, she couldn't get her anger under control. She counted to one hundred very slowly, but that only seemed to make her madder. She couldn't take any more. She was ready to bust.

Seamus pulled up next to the rear steps of the veranda and Connell got out. He reached for her, but Leah slapped his hands away. She slid from the truck, slammed the door behind her, and stomped up the steps and into the house. She went to the coffeepot and set it up to make a fresh pot. She slammed cupboards and drawers as she worked. Large hands on her waist had her spinning around, and she pushed against Connell's chest with all her might. It pissed her off even more when he only took a step back, and she knew he had done that and it hadn't been from her effort to push him away.

"What the fuck is wrong with you, Leah? You've been snapping and snarling around here for the last few days and I've just about had all I can take," Connell stated in a steely voice.

"You've had enough?" Leah replied coldly to Connell. "I have had it up to here with you and Seamus doing everything for me. I am not a fucking piece of fragile glass. I can't even make a coffee without getting the third degree. I have just had the all clear from the doctor, so you and your brother can just go back to your ranch work and leave me the hell alone.

"Do you know how embarrassed I was with you and your brother asking so many intimate questions about me, as if I wasn't there? God, you make me so mad I could scream."

"You are screaming, darlin'," Seamus said from behind Connell.

"Don't you start. I've had it with you two. If I want a glass of water, it's in my hand before I can even get up to get it. You have given me everything I've needed without question but you're driving me crazy. It has to stop and it's stopping right now," Leah stated.

"I agree, baby. It's stopping right now." Connell growled in his deep, lyrical voice.

Leah looked up to Connell and knew she probably looked like an idiot with her mouth hanging open, but he had surprised the shit out of her when he had agreed with her. Connell moved a step toward her, then another, and another until he had her crowded against the countertop. He placed his arms on either side of her, leaning on his hands, effectively caging her in. He looked down into her eyes, and she bit her lip to hold in the moan bubbling up in her chest.

"What?"

"I said, we're not going to be treating you like fragile glass anymore, baby. We were just waiting for Doc's all clear before we backed off. Now that he has pronounced you fit and healthy, you're in big trouble," Connell said.

Leah gasped when Connell leaned down, slanting his mouth over hers. He devoured her like a man dying of thirst. He gave no quarter. He used his soft yet firm lips to pry hers apart and swept his tongue into the recess of her mouth. He thrust and retreated, parried and conquered her tongue with his, until she was a big pool of liquid desire. She felt her legs shaking and knew she was in danger of her knees buckling. She reached up and wrapped her arms around Connell's neck. She clung to him, lost in a world of desire.

He withdrew his mouth from hers, and she was pleased to note she wasn't the only one breathing heavily. His eyes were glittering down at her, and she should have gone up in flames from the heat she could see there. He moved back, easing his hands from around her waist, and moved off to the side to give his brother access to her.

Leah turned her head and saw the same heated look on Seamus's face as was on Connell's. Seamus picked her up into his arms and slammed his mouth down over hers. Her world spun literally as well as figuratively as Seamus ravished her mouth and carried her from the room.

Chapter Eighteen

Seamus carried Leah down the hall to their bedroom. He placed her on the mattress, but instead of letting her go, he followed her down and covered her with his body. He had been waiting for this day for over two weeks, and he was so horny he was shaking with it. He knew Connell was in the same predicament as he was, and if he had to guess at the cause of Leah's bitching over the last few days, she was suffering from sexual frustration as well. Now that Doc had given Leah the all clear, there were no holds barred.

Seamus groaned as Leah slid and twirled her tongue around his. He had missed this with her, missed the intimate connection of the body and soul he felt when he was having sex with the woman he loved more than his own life. He weaned his mouth from hers and moved off to the side. He reached for the buttons on her shirt and began to undo them. He saw Connell crawl onto the bed at the bottom and reach for the waistband of her jeans. Between his and Connell's ministrations they had Leah naked within moments. The sight of her luscious curves and warm, creamy skin made his cock jerk in his pants. Her dusky, rosy nipples were hard and pointing toward the ceiling. He leaned over her and took the nipple closest to him into his mouth and suckled on her. He took her other nipple between his finger and thumb and began to pluck at the turgid peak. He opened his eyes and looked down to see his brother licking at Leah's pussy. Judging by the slurping sounds he was making, Leah was creaming copious amounts of juices.

* * * *

Connell couldn't get enough of Leah's cream. He lapped at her cunt and stabbed his tongue into her pussy hole. He rubbed her clit with the tip of his finger and slurped up all of her juices. He swallowed down as much of her cum as he could and worked her sweet little pussy for more. He was so turned on by the feel of her beneath his hands and mouth, the sweet, musky smell of her cunt, and the taste of her on his tongue that his cock was jumping in his pants and he was shaking. He wanted to give his woman at least one orgasm before he buried his cock into her depths, but he didn't know if he could hold off that long.

The sounds emitting from Leah's mouth were driving him wild, and the way she bucked and twisted beneath him was only making it harder for him to hold back. He removed his finger from her clit and slid his tongue up between her wet folds. He licked over her clit with the tip of his tongue and thrust two fingers into her tight, wet sheath. He twisted his fingers around in her body until his palm was faceup, and he began to pump his fingers in and out of her until she was pushing her hips up into his mouth. He caged her clit between his teeth and flicked the little nub with his tongue over and over again. He slid his fingers in and out of her twat, making sure to slide the pads over the rough, spongy place inside her. He chuckled against her clit with male pride and satisfaction when he felt her walls closing in on his fingers until she was gripping his digits as tight as a fist.

He could hear her keening in the back of her throat and knew she was about to go over the edge and reach nirvana. He hooked his fingers inside her and gave a gentle but firm tug, and she screamed. The sound of Leah screaming his and Seamus's names had him nearly coming in his pants as she covered his hand with her liquid release. He enhanced her pleasure by rubbing inside her until the last quiver of her internal muscles faded away. He withdrew his hand, licked his fingers clean, rose from the bed, and shucked his clothes. He was between her splayed thighs again before she had her breath back.

Connell aimed for Leah's cunt and buried his cock balls-deep into her body. He moaned but held still a moment, savoring her tight, wet walls gripping his erection and also giving her time to adjust to having his hard penis embedded in her. He slid his hands beneath her ass, gripped her fleshy globes, tilting her pelvis up, and began to pump his dick in and out of her pussy. He was home, and he never wanted to leave. He thrust a few more times, then stilled again, his cock buried to the hilt. He slid his hand up beneath her back, moved his legs, and brought her up onto his lap. He and Leah both moaned at the same time when his penis moved in another inch. He could feel the head of his cock butting up against her cervix.

"Are you all right, baby? Am I hurting you?" Connell panted out.

"No. I need you to fuck me, Connell."

"We have to let Seamus get in your ass first, baby. Then we are gonna fuck you so good." Connell growled as he shoved his hips up.

"A little cold, darlin'," Seamus said from behind Leah.

"Hold still and let Seamus prepare your ass, baby. Don't tense up, relax those muscles. Good girl," Connell crooned.

Connell couldn't believe how tight Leah's cunt got when Seamus shoved his fingers up her ass. He could feel his brother's fingers stretching and pumping in and out of Leah's back door through the thin membrane of flesh separating her anus and pussy. He couldn't wait for Seamus to shove his cock into Leah's little pucker. He knew she got even tighter when he and his brother fucked her at the same time.

"Easy, darlin', just breathe deeply for me. That's it. You're doing fine, Leah. Use those muscles and push me out. Oh yeah, darlin', you feel so good," Seamus groaned. "I'm in, sweetheart. My cock is all the way in your ass."

Connell could feel Leah's walls rippling around his dick and knew he couldn't stay still any longer. He had to move. He gripped Leah's ribs and pulled his cock out of her tight sheath until his cockhead was resting in the entrance of her hole. As he pushed back in, he felt

Seamus pull out of her ass. They set up a slow rhythm of slide and glide, push and retreat, in and out, gaining depth and speed with every forward thrust of their hips.

The sound of Leah whimpering and mewling as her cunt rippled and gripped him had him unleashing his control. He began to pound in and out her pussy, his cock sliding in and out easily as she bathed his hard rod with her juices. Her pussy slurped around his flesh as he slammed his hips against hers, the friction of their flesh sliding against each other absolute bliss.

He and Seamus were now fucking her at the same time. Both he and Seamus filled her and withdrew together, giving her the ultimate pleasure they could ever offer their woman. Leah rocked her hips back and forth between them, trying to control her own pleasure. Connell was having none of that. It was his and his brother's duty to see that she reached climax, not hers.

Connell nodded to Seamus over Leah's shoulder, and between them they picked her up off the bed and stood. They had her hanging between them, her arms wrapped around his neck as she clung to him, and he saw Seamus slide his arms beneath her knees, holding her legs out wide. They fucked her like there was no tomorrow.

Connell bent his knees and slammed his pelvis into Leah. She cried out and threw her head back, her face slack with pleasure. He and Seamus rocked their hips into her then retreated, gliding their dicks into and out of her ass and pussy over and over again. He could feel her shaking in his arms and knew she was close to her peak. With the next surge of his hips he twisted his pelvis and ground his pubic bone into her clit. She went wild between them. She screamed long and loud, her Kegel muscles clamped down on his cock, held on for a moment, then released him again. Her internal walls rippled, clenched, and contracted around his erection over and over, and he knew he was a goner.

Connell felt the tingle at the base of his spine travel around to his contracting balls. His testicles drew up tight to his body, and then he was roaring out as he cock shot off load after load of semen. He heard Seamus's voice join in the cacophony and knew his brother had just found his own release. Connell's legs shook so much he sank down to the floor, taking Leah and his brother with him. He sat there on the floor, the love of his life wrapped in his arms and clinging to his neck as he tried to get his breath and strength back. He nuzzled her neck and placed a kiss on her shoulder.

"Do you feel better now, baby?" Connell asked.

"Yeah," Leah sighed.

"Do you want a bath, darlin'?" Seamus asked from behind Leah.

"Yeah."

"Is that all you can say after we just loved on you, baby?" Connell asked with a snicker.

"Yeah," Leah answered then laughed. "Wait, no. I mean. Oh shit, you've fried my brain."

Connell chuckled then gently withdrew his cock from her pussy. He picked her up in his arms, stumbled as his wobbly legs protested, then carried her into the bathroom.

"When can we do that again?" Leah asked.

"After we have some lunch, baby. Let me get a shower and then I'll get some food. Seamus will help you with your bath."

"I don't need help to bathe. I have been doing it for a long time, you know," Leah replied.

"I know you have, darlin'. But we like taking care of you," Seamus replied.

"I don't want you waiting on me hand and foot anymore. I'm perfectly fine to do things for myself now."

"We know you are, baby. And we will back off now that Doc has given you the all clear," Connell stated as he reached in and turned the shower on.

"Really? Then why is Seamus bathing me?"

"'Cos we like touching you any chance we can get, darlin'," Seamus replied.

"Okay, I suppose I can deal with you wanting to touch me," Leah said, deadpan. "As long as I can touch you anytime I want."

"We're all yours, baby. Anytime you want to touch you just go right ahead," Connell called from the shower.

He watched as Leah leaned back against the rim of the tub while his brother washed their woman. She was so gorgeous with her nipples peeking out from above the water, her white, creamy skin and flushed cheeks. He turned away and concentrated on washing himself. He was getting hard again already. He needed food for the next round, and he wanted to give Leah a chance to recover before he and Seamus made love to her again. Once done, he turned off the shower, dried off, and hurried from the bathroom.

He was eager to start round two.

Epilogue

Leah sat in the kitchen drinking a glass of juice as she talked with Debbie. It had been six months since Debbie's ex Shayne had nearly killed Leah, and they had become fast friends. Debbie had set up her lingerie shop and was living in the apartment above the store.

Leah breathed deeply as her stomach churned when the juice hit her belly and knew she was going to be ill. The sickness hit her at the oddest times. It was never first thing in the morning, but it seemed that anything too acidic didn't agree with her. She shot off her chair and made it to the bathroom with moments to spare.

"Are you okay, Leah? Do you want me to call Connell and Seamus?" Debbie asked.

"No. I'm fine. For goodness' sake don't call those two and tell them I'm sick. They'd have me in bed for a week if they knew."

"That bad, huh?" Debbie questioned.

"Worse," Leah replied with a grimace then hung her head over the toilet bowl again. When Leah was done, she brushed her teeth, rinsed her mouth with mouthwash, and headed back to the kitchen.

"Did I tell you I found out why Earl was such an asshole to work for?" Leah asked.

"No, so tell me."

"It turns out Earl is my half-brother. My mom had an affair with his dad and no one knew but Earl's parents and my mom. He apparently found out after his parents left town. He was going through a box his parents left behind and found a letter from my mom to his dad. Even though he was always mean to me, he was even worse when he found out we were related. Apparently he was disgusted because he had asked me out before he knew. Thank God I didn't like him and never accepted. The thought of what could have happened just turns my stomach," Leah explained.

"Eew, that is so gross. Any wonder you were sick," Debbie replied.

Leah didn't answer but couldn't contain her grin and unconsciously rubbed her belly. Debbie had obviously seen her action and put two and two together.

"So when are you going to tell your husbands you're expecting?" Debbie asked with a smile.

"About an hour before I give birth," Leah answered quickly then laughed. "I hear you've had two men hanging around the shop lately. Want to tell me about that?"

"Not really," Debbie replied.

"I hear they're good men, Deb. Britt and Daniel Delaney have worked for the government for quite a few years in a special-operatives branch that is not on paper. They really have the hots for you."

"I've had enough of men to last me a lifetime. There is no way I'm getting involved with those two," Debbie stated.

"They're really hot, aren't they?" Leah stated more than asked and watched with satisfaction as her friend got a soft, sappy look on her face.

"Yes, they're gorgeous. Oh shit, you're such a sneaky bitch," Deb replied with a laugh. "Have you seen how friggin' huge Britt is? That man scares me to death whenever he comes near me. What is worse is you don't even know he's there until he's standing right in front of you. He makes me jump every time."

"I'll bet your panties are wet just thinking about them," Leah said with a snicker.

"You are so bad," Deb replied with a laugh, and Leah saw her look over behind her. "So when are you due?"

"Leah. Are you okay, baby?" Connell said as he rushed to her side and swept her up into his arms. "When did you find out you were pregnant? Are you feeling sick?"

"Bitch," Leah mouthed over Connell's head as he cuddled up to her.

"Back at ya," Debbie replied. "I'm leaving, don't see me out. I see you have your hands full."

Debbie waved to her and left without once looking back. Leah was going to have to figure out a way to get Britt and Daniel Delaney together with her friend. She just knew they would be so good for her. But for now she had two men to take care of, and that was just the way she liked it.

She had married her men in a small private ceremony three months previously and now she was expecting their baby. She knew she was going to have to work at keeping her husbands from treating her as if she was ill instead of pregnant, but she wouldn't have had it any other way.

She loved Connell and Seamus and knew they loved her. She was even going to learn to tolerate them mollycoddling her but only to a certain extent. She knew they only did it because they cared so much for her. She couldn't wait to hold the baby they had made together in her arms and share in the joy of raising her husbands' children. She was looking forward to the next fifty or so years of her life with her men by her side.

She wrapped her arms around Connell's neck as he carried her toward the bedroom. She heard the door slam and footsteps racing up the hall behind. It looked like she was going to have a very relaxing afternoon. She loved it when her husbands played hooky and they whiled away the hours making love with her.

THE END

WWW.BECCAVAN-EROTICROMANCE.COM

ABOUT THE AUTHOR

My name is Becca Van. I live in Australia with my wonderful hubby of many years, as well as my children, a pigeon pair, (a girl and a boy). I have always wanted to write and last year decided to do just that.

I didn't want to stay in the mainstream of a boring nine-to-five job, so I quit, fulfilling my passion for writing. I decided to utilize my time with something I knew I would enjoy and had always wanted to do. I submitted my first manuscript to Siren-BookStrand a few months ago, and much to my excited delight, I got a reply saying they would love to publish my story. I literally jump out of bed with excitement each day and can't wait for my laptop to power up so I can get to work.

Also by Becca Van

Ménage Everlasting: Slick Rock 1: *Slick Rock Cowboys*
Ménage Everlasting: Slick Rock 2: *Double E Ranch*
Ménage Everlasting: Slick Rock 3: *Her Ex-Marines*
Ménage Everlasting: Slick Rock 5: *Her Shadow Men*
Ménage Everlasting: Slick Rock 6: *Her Personal Security*

For all other titles, please visit
www.bookstrand.com/becca-van

Siren Publishing, Inc.
www.SirenPublishing.com

CPSIA information can be obtained at www.ICGtesting.com
Printed in the USA
BVOW012224230712

296005BV00007B/18/P